Praise for *Can you hear me?*

'*Can you hear me?* poignantly touches on problems
of friendships, families and coming-of-age in
a small community in northern Italy. There is
much beauty and sadness in this slim novel.'
Times

'The novel is carried by both the brilliance of its
setting and by a scattering of emotional truths . . . It is
refreshing to read a novel of crime and darkness that
eschews straightforward domestic noir, and Varvello
was brave to write about the trauma that haunts her.'
Guardian

'Move over Ferrante, there's a new Elena in town . . .
The novel is something akin to noir, but the emphasis
is on the psychological . . . It made me think of the
opening of Ian McEwan's *The Cement Garden*.'
Independent

'A claustrophobic read . . . Marrying the unsettling feelings
of a coming-of-age tale with a panic-inducing abduction
story, Varvello explores the psychological impacts of
fear, love and mental illness in pared-back prose.'
Daily Express

'Varvello is emerging as one of the strongest young
voices in the Italian literary world . . . a bleak and
vivid book, about the way that life can throw up
events that are forever impossible to come to terms
with, so that subsequent life is a joyless affair.'
TLS

'A taut, smart, viciously gripping noir about family and the destructive force of unconditional love. It took my breath away and kept me glued to the page until its heart-breaking end: a phenomenal achievement.'
Kirsty Wark, author of
The Legacy Of Elizabeth Pringle

'A beautiful, stark, poignant account of fear, love and loss.'
Emma Flint, author of *Little Deaths*

'I loved Varvello's pared-back writing style, and how she manages to say so much in so few words. An intense read, wonderfully anxiety-inducing, where everything is bubbling uneasily just below the surface.'
Claire Fuller, author of *Our Endless Numbered Days*

'Haunting, surreal, and deeply engaging, Elena Varvello's *Can you hear me?* is at once suspenseful and elegiac, as beautiful as it is horrifying, as Varvello takes us deep inside the mind and heart of 16-year-old Elia Furenti during his summer of change. Readers will devour this novel in one sitting as I did, then chew over it long after the book is done.'
Karen Dionne, author of
The Marsh King's Daughter

'*Can you hear me?* shines a light on one family's black heart, a place where opposites coexist: tenderness and fear; happiness and pain; unfaltering faith and ugly suspicions. A book to get lost in.'
Paolo Giordano, bestselling author of
The Solitude of Prime Numbers

Can you hear me?

Elena Varvello

Translated by Alex Valente

Supported using public funding by
ARTS COUNCIL
ENGLAND

This book has been selected to receive financial assistance from English PEN's "PEN Translates" programme, supported by Arts Council England. English PEN exists to promote literature and our understanding of it, to uphold writers' freedoms around the world, to campaign against the persecution and imprisonment of writers for stating their views, and to promote the friendly co-operation of writers and the free exchange of ideas. www.englishpen.org

First published in Great Britain in 2017 by Two Roads
An imprint of John Murray Press
An Hachette UK company

First published in Italy in 2016 by Einaudi Editore

This paperback edition published in 2018

2

A CIP catalogue record for this title is available from the British Library

Paperback ISBN 978 1 473 65489 1
Ebook ISBN 978 1 473 65490 7
Audio Digital Download 978 1 47 366564 4

Typeset in Sabon MT by Hewer Text UK Ltd, Edinburgh
Printed and bound in Great Britain by Clays Ltd, Elcograf S.p.A.

Hodder & Stoughton policy is to use papers that are natural, renewable and recyclable products and made from wood grown in sustainable forests. The logging and manufacturing processes are expected to conform to the environmental regulations of the country of origin.

Hodder & Stoughton Ltd
Carmelite House
50 Victoria Embankment
London EC4Y 0DZ

www.hodder.co.uk
www.tworoadsbooks.com

In talking about the past we lie
with every breath we draw.
William Maxwell

Can you hear me?

In the Woods

In the August of 1978, the summer I met Anna Trabuio, my father took a girl into the woods.

He stopped the van at the side of the road, just before sunset, asked her where she was going, and told her to get in.

She accepted the lift because she knew him.

They saw him drive towards town with his lights off, then he left the road, took a steep and difficult path and made her get out, he dragged her along with him.

My mother and I waited for him, worried he might've had an accident. While I stared into the darkness from the lounge window, she made a few phone calls.

'He's still not back.'

I found her leaning against the wall, in the hallway, the receiver clutched against her chest.

'Everything's fine, you'll see,' she said, trying to smile, as if she'd just heard his van, his footsteps in the yard.

She phoned the nearest hospital: she sighed with relief when they told her he wasn't there.

She put some coffee on and we sat down at the kitchen table. She was wearing a blue dress, with long sleeves, dotted with small green palm trees that looked on the verge of being violently uprooted by an unstoppable wind.

'Don't worry,' she said.

I went back to the lounge, lay down on the sofa and dozed off, a confused sleep that didn't last long.

My mother was in the yard. 'Why don't you go to bed?' she asked.

'Not tired any more.'

She reached over to hug my shoulders and looked up to the sky: 'Look how clear it is.'

'Are you cold?' I asked.

It was a summer night, and she was shaking.

She went to lie down and I tried reading a comic.

Half an hour later she left her room. She was wearing a blanket over her shoulders. She shook her head: 'It's pointless, I can't rest.' She went to the bathroom, then went back into the kitchen and called me. 'Do you want to stay with me for a bit?' She pulled the blanket up to her chin.

Before dawn, through the silence, we heard his van.

She turned towards the door, straightened her back, shook off the blanket and ran her hand through her hair. 'Oh thank goodness. Thank God.' I watched as she got up, straightened her dress on her hips and headed outside: 'Darling, what happened to you?'

I followed right behind her. I stayed on the porch, under the light, trying to make him out in the darkness. I was angry and relieved: I wanted to slap him and tell him I didn't care – *you could've just stayed there*; I wanted to run over to him and make sure he wasn't hurt.

They stepped into the light, slowly, and I watched them go inside.

I was sixteen.

He had been gone a long time already, but that was it – not even a year after he lost his job and that boy disappeared – that was when everything broke.

Truth (1)

Can you hear me?

I remember his voice, at night.

Waking up all of a sudden, that summer, I'd hear the water going in the bathroom, my father's steps in the corridor, him coughing. My mother kept calling him: 'Come to bed.' He'd reply: 'No time.'

He'd head down to the garage, or sit at the kitchen table.

I'd fall asleep again.

On one of those nights I heard my father's breathing from the other side of my bedroom door.

I stayed as still as possible, listening. He came inside.

'Elia?'

The light was on behind him.

'Elia, can you hear me?'

I opened my eyes very slightly. I wanted to ask him: *What is it, Dad? What's going on with you?* Instead, I turned the other way, pretending to sleep, pulling the covers over my head.

My father's name, the low and gravelly voice with which he said it: 'My name is Ettore Furenti.'

My mother adored him. I'd often catch her admiring him, her chin on her hand, a smile across her lips.

'Your father is so beautiful. And he always makes me laugh.'

And he *was* fun: his laughter was contagious, and he had a whole collection of stories he liked to tell.

'Elia? Come here a second.'

'What is it?'

'You need to hear this one.'

A big, bulky man, wide forehead, black hair and eyes of a watery blue – she was small, tiny, and always cold, chestnut hair and eyes. I can still see how he'd hold her against him, just back from work, with his coat still on, both so young: they turn and smile as they catch me watching them. I see them walking into the bedroom, my mother's head only just up to his shoulder, and he winks at me, closing the door.

In summer, on Sundays, he'd take me to the river for a swim, or to the cinema – his profile against clouds of smoke, in the dimmed lights, and the way he'd start whistling as we left, and say: 'Let's play a trick on her when we get home.' He'd make the turn onto our drive, roll down to the garage and carefully close the car doors, chuckling, and she'd know what we had in mind, but still exclaimed: 'I wonder when they'll be back.' He'd grab her by the waist and kiss her neck and she'd shriek then burst into laughter.

'You scared me.'

'His fault' – he'd point at me – 'it was his idea.'

But there were moments when he'd change, and he'd lock himself in the garage and we were not to disturb him. He'd sit under the porch canopy, on the swing, for hours, wringing his hands, biting his lips. I caught him sobbing, one after-noon – everything was still fine then – sitting in the bathtub, pale and shivering, with his knees clutched to his chest.

When he was particularly tired or worried, he'd stut-ter: he'd pause, shake his head, hit his thigh with his closed fist.

He could freeze in a second – she never was able to do the same – and become cold and sarcastic; he'd stare at us as if we were wrong somehow, his lips curled in a sneer; then everything would go back to normal and I'd hear them muttering, I'd hear my father's laugh.

I knew very little about his past.

He had lost his parents at eighteen, within three months of each other. No other relatives, just like her. One summer, before they died, he'd worked as a mechanic at the petrol station, and after that he was employed at the plant.

'I don't remember much,' he'd answer, whenever I tried asking him about it.

He often went out with my mother – into town for a stroll, or a coffee, or for a meal at *Il cacciatore*, along the road that zigzagged through the woods, leading to our house and that of Ida Belli – but he had no friends and never showed signs of missing anyone.

'I need no one.'

I'd ask her, sometimes, what he'd been like when he was younger.

'Pretty much the same as now.'

A funny man, I'd tell myself, armed with quick comebacks. It was always an odd sight to find him on the porch, staring at the garden and the woods in silence, or locked up in the garage.

My mother, on the other hand, had Ida, and she loved her.

'She's like a sister.'

She was a tall woman, short hair, sharp jaw, quite brusque and with a horsey laugh; she could suddenly strangle you with a hug, or slap a hand on your shoulder.

She had divorced her husband, he had moved to Rome and married again. She lived with her daughter, whom we still treated as a child, despite her being my age – some people thought she had some type of disability, with her slumped back, her big dangling head, her damp, puckered lips.

Ida would always say: 'We get on perfectly just the two of us, Simona and me.'

I always remember the girl standing behind her mother's shoulders, mumbling and chewing on my name. It was practically impossible to touch her without her screaming or moaning, and she didn't attend school: she spent her time drawing, kneeling on the ground, smearing colours all over her face whenever something worried her.

Ida, an accountant for the local furniture factory, had employed a girl full-time, to look after her daughter.

The girl came up every morning, on the bus, and left late afternoon, shuffling quickly to the bus stop, cigarette in hand, as the light disappeared behind the trees.

Until she met my father.

We lived at the top of a hill – the house where he grew up – where the road died into a path, three kilometres from Ponte, a small provincial town we used to call 'the city' because of the mill. A narrow valley, an abandoned pyrite mine, a twisting river, an old stone bridge in the gorge, another with two lanes over the river and woods all around. But there were also schools, the *Futura* cinema, the public library – my mother's realm, as the sole librarian – a café with a video-game arcade. There was the furniture factory, including a kitchen-and-wardrobe showroom, in the area we called 'industrial'. And the mill, with the brick wall around it, the chimney smoke.

It was a cotton mill, which had been founded in 1939 and had flourished since then. Two hundred employees at the end of the 1960s. My father was a repairman, he loved his job and wouldn't have changed it for anything.

Once orders started to fall and prices to rise, the company was sold. My father used to tell us: 'The wind is changing.' The new owners meddled with the books, stole some money, tricked people. In 1977, they declared bankruptcy. I saw him cry that day – it was September – as my mother sat next to him, consoling him.

All that was left was the brick wall with the broken-bottle glass on top. The cold chimneys. The whistling between the empty buildings.

In the months that followed we had fun climbing over the wall – me and a group of kids I used to hang out with back then. We broke in through the doors. We threw stones at the windows and turned over filing cabinets. We peed against walls and wrote lewd graffiti on them. We sat on the floor, next to the machines, in the dusty shadows, sharing a cigarette. We spent time in that wide, silent space, as if it were ours.

Then suddenly we got bored of it – in December, after that boy disappeared.

Back then my father used to go out every day, but I had no idea where.

*   *   *

The fall of the mill was the beginning of the end.

It had been a disaster for Ponte. Many left, looking for work. Several others started drinking, or just loitering.

My father locked himself in his bedroom for weeks, only getting up to go to the bathroom or join us in the kitchen, in his pyjamas, when my mother called him for food. He'd stare at the plate with a cigarette between his lips, and my mother would remove it, softly.

'We'll survive this, you'll see.'

'How?'

'Later. Eat first.'

My mother asked around – the factory, a construction company – but no one had any openings. Then she found out about a piece of land, bought by some company, about twenty kilometres from Ponte, where a small housing complex was supposed to go up.

'Maybe something'll come out of it.'

She would lie down next to him whenever she got back from the library, and that's how I remember them, one next to the other, almost indistinguishable, despite their stark differences.

Holed up in his room, he came up with an idea, he fixated on it.

He came to the table one day, filled his glass with water, drank some, and said: 'I've had time to think.'

My mother looked at him, and her eyes lit up. 'About what?'

How could she know?

'They found a way to get rid of me,' he replied. 'That's what they wanted. And now they're mocking me.'

'It's happened to everyone, sweetheart.'

My father's lips curled into a bitter smile. 'That's what they're telling us. But it's not the truth.' He moved his chair, and went back to the bedroom.

I turned towards her. 'What did he mean?'

'Nothing, it's nothing.'

My father said the same thing the following evening, and the one after that, and for weeks afterwards. He called it a 'conspiracy' once, stabbing his index finger hard onto the table: 'a full-on plan, all just a show.'

'I should've listened,' he said.

'To whom?' asked my mother.

'I can't tell you.'

'You're just a little confused. I know this is hard.'

'No. No, you don't.'

One morning, he woke up before dawn and headed to the garage – a worktop, a metal cabinet, a sink, a small, dirty, broken couch, an electric heater.

That was where I found him when I got home: barefoot, in his grey pyjamas, scribbling busily on some paper.

'What are you doing?'

'Nothing. Where have *you* been?'

'School,' I said. He knew that.

He folded the paper in half, fished out a cigarette from its packet and started smoking.

'What are you writing?'

My father didn't reply: he stared at a point somewhere behind my shoulders, beyond the open door, to the white autumn sky.

'It's cold,' I said. 'At least turn on the heater.'

'I'm OK.'

'Have you been here since this morning?'

'I don't want to sleep any more.'

'Do you want me to bring you a jumper?'

'I said I'm OK.'

'OK.'

'I'll sort things out,' he said, finally. 'Don't you worry.'

I should've insisted. What had got into him? Did he really believe the other employees were still working, that the mill was still running? But instead I just let him be, left him to his ghosts, believing he was safe.

He went out to buy envelopes and stamps.

'So is it letters?' my mother asked him. 'Who are you sending them to?'

'Everyone needs to know about this,' he replied.

She sighed: 'It's pointless. Whatever this is.'

'You don't understand. I need to report them. They need to take me back.'

She brushed his cheek, his hand. 'No one can take you back, sweetheart. There's no one left. You know what happened.'

My father looked at her and bit his lip, eyes half shut, as if thinking hard about something.

'You do know, right? Ettore, please tell me you do.'

'That's the point. What is the truth?'

'There's only one truth,' she replied.

'Are you sure?'

He spent that night – his first one fully awake – in front of the TV, staring at the static of the test card. At one point I went to the bathroom to pee. As I headed back to my room, I heard him mutter: 'Fine, I'll keep my mouth shut.'

Can you hear me?

Two weeks later, on a Sunday, he told us about the van.

He wasn't home when my mother and I got up for breakfast. I asked her where he was, and she shook her head. We heard the car a couple of minutes later. My father stepped into the kitchen, threw his coat onto a chair, rubbed his cold hands together, and took off his shoes.

'There's a guy selling his van. I told him I'll buy it.'

My mother asked him who the man was.

'You don't know him.'

'Come on, everyone knows everyone around here. How much?' They had talked, on and off, about a second car, but he was unemployed at the time, and the whole of my mother's salary went on bills and groceries.

'It's none of your business,' he said.

'I think it is.'

'You live here, don't you?'

'So?'

'So this is my house, and I think I should be the one making the decisions.' He turned towards me, stretched across the table and tugged at the sleeve of my pyjama top. 'Isn't it a great idea?'

He burst out laughing, then went over to my mother, grabbed her by the waist, hoisted her up. She tried to wrestle away from him, saying 'You can't do things like this.' But she eventually gave in.

It was early December. The wind was icy cold.

'I feel like a god. Don't argue with me.'

He twirled her between the table and the door, and she grabbed onto his back, and they kissed.

So he bought the van.

I slid on my coat and went out, that afternoon, the light of dusk, when I heard the horn beeping. My father was sitting there, hands on the steering wheel. He lowered the window and called me over. 'Come see,' he said.

I walked around the van and eventually got in.

'So? What do you think?'

I shrugged.

I didn't like it: there was a dent on the right-hand side, and spots where the white paint had been eaten by rust. The inside smelled bad. It had not been a good deal.

He drummed his fingers on the wheel, staring at the windscreen. 'You know what they did,' he said.

'Who?'

'Them.'

We sat in silence for a bit.

'Your mother doesn't believe me. I can't trust her any more.'

'What should she believe?'

'I told you: all of this,' he replied, leaning towards me. Then he muttered, 'But I'm writing those letters.'

'Who to?'

'Everyone.'

'And you're sending them?'

'What else would they be for?'

'Can I read a few?'

'Absolutely not.'

'Why not?'

'Not yet. One day.' He ruffled my hair, opened the door and started getting out. 'Never let them trick you, Elia. Remember that.'

He started taking the van out every morning, coming back after dark; he let his beard grow and shaved off his hair. He became restless: he never stopped talking, stuttering, getting lost in confused conversations we were no longer able to follow. And he kept spending his nights on the sofa, seated at the table, or pacing the hallway back and forth.

Then that child disappeared, Giorgio Longhi – he was on his way home from school – and everyone started looking for him, and us kids headed for the river, without our parents knowing, our eyes on the rapids, on the livid water, on the branches pressing against the concrete pylons. We walked down a couple of paths, looking in the bushes, stamping on piles of leaves. 'How much do we get if we find him?', 'You asshole, what does it matter?', 'We get him home first, then we'll see'.

Two days went by. It snowed.

Carabinieri and local police combed the streets again, some of the ruins in the fields and the plant, then they headed for the woods. I saw one of their cars, sirens on, zooming across the bridge.

An article in the *Eco della Valle* ran his photo: mouth open in a smile, eyes half closed but alert.

I found two copies of the paper in our garage, next to the toolbox. I took one and looked at it, folded open to that page, the boy's photo. My father came home – I didn't notice him – came into the garage, walked towards me and snatched it out of my hands.

He was dripping wet, his work shoes and trousers both filthy. His teeth were chattering.

I thought he might've joined the search parties, or been looking alone, in the snow, hoping to find him, but when I asked he shook his head.

'I'm on guard duty,' he said.

'Where?'

He put down the newspapers on a shelf, pulled out a folded piece of paper and waved it under the neon light, then scrunched it up in his fist. 'It says so here,' he replied. He rubbed his forehead. 'Do you want to know what I remembered?'

'Yes.'

'Listen to me,' he said, then he told me about a man he had met, when he was much younger. The man had a dog, he told me, and was convinced the dog talked to him and suggested he did things. 'They thought he'd gone mad.'

'No kidding. Then what happened?'

'I can't remember.' He put the crumpled paper back in his pocket and went over to sit on the sofa. 'These are my things, down here. Don't come rummaging.'

'I wasn't.'

'Leave now,' he said. 'And turn off that light.'

My mother and I had dinner, watched TV, then went to bed. My father did not join us. At a certain point in the night I woke up – a loud thud. Another. And another.

I heard my mother leave her room, running down to the garage. 'Oh Lord, you're bleeding. Let me see, come here.'

He started yelling. 'Were you in it too? Were you? Tell me.'

The conspiracy again. And all his letters.

I got out of bed, opened the door slowly, stepped into

the hallway. They came from the garage and switched on the light. I pressed my eyes shut and when I opened them again I saw my father holding his wrist, his right hand bleeding. My mother with untidy, electric hair.

'Dad? What happened?'

He looked at me, licking his lips. 'What the fuck do you want?' he replied, and kicked the telephone stand.

'Go back to sleep, Elia,' she told me.

They locked themselves away in the kitchen.

'Are you happy now?' I heard him say. 'You see what you make me do?'

'Please, hold still.'

When I fell asleep again, I found myself on the river-bank, next to that kid. *They were looking for you*, I told him, *and so was I. You knew I was here*, he replied, *that's why you came.*

The following morning – my father was collapsed on the sofa, snoring with his mouth open, bandages on his hand – I found the newspapers cut into pieces, scissors next to them, blood on the front door. Only one photo of the boy remained intact: I took it, slipped back into my room, and hid it in a drawer.

My mother didn't speak of that night again and my father seemed to calm down, as if he had been able to douse a fire that had threatened to burn him.

He became quiet, his hand swollen and purple. He

shaved his beard, let his hair grow out, went back to using his bed.

I often thought about what had happened – the thuds and his yelling – and I was always wary. Restless. I stopped going out with the other kids: maybe their fathers drank, or sometimes beat them, or perhaps they unloaded their frustration on their children or their wives, but they never believed in conspiracies and wrote to no one.

I'd stay in my room for hours, reading comics.

I snuck cigarettes out of the packets he'd leave around and smoked them behind the house when my mother was at work, sitting on my heels, back against the wall, shaking from the cold, then I'd go to the bathroom and brush my teeth.

I saw them in the yard one afternoon – a blue wound on the horizon – while they were decorating a small, skinny pine tree with coloured balls.

'What do you think?' my mother asked.

He touched his injured hand, picked up the box with the decorations from on top of the van, took it back to the garage.

She joined me on the porch. 'It's because of your father, isn't it?'

'What?'

'You're always alone these days.' She stamped her boots clean, slipped off her woollen gloves, touched her hair. 'It was a bad dream, Elia, but he's awake now.'

She took my chin between her fingers, looked me in the eyes and smiled, then went into the kitchen.

Then they found the boy – next to the pyrite mine, at the foot of a drop, buried in snow, completely naked, hands and feet tied with shoelaces.

They had kidnapped him, choked him.

Ponte was invaded by reporters and camera crews, several articles were published, they even talked about it on national TV. My mother and I watched the report from the sofa, with the lights off. Red and white tape hanging between the trees. Parents in tears, standing between two *carabinieri*. The smiling face, the one from the photo, appeared on the screen.

She covered her mouth with her hand. 'Who could possibly have done something like that?'

My father came into the lounge and stopped behind us.

'Ettore,' she said, 'this isn't possible.'

She reached out an arm and touched him, sniffing. I turned round: my father's face, tense in that liquid light.

'It's not possible,' she said again.

I saw him purse his lips, as he stared at the TV. 'Why don't you open your eyes, Marta?'

On Christmas Day, they gave me a sweater, a new cassette player and two tapes.

'Dad chose them,' she told me.

He hinted at a smile. She rested her head against his arm.

Ida and Simona had dinner with us. 'Let's try celebrating, even at a time as sad as this.' Simona never stopped drawing, circles and spirals, paper and pens next to her plate.

Later, I found my father out on the porch, on the swing chair, holding a cup of coffee. I was wearing my new jumper.

'Come here a moment,' he said. 'Sit.' He made room for me. 'It suits you. The top.'

'Thanks.'

He stared in silence at the snow mounds, his van, the empty sky with no stars. He squeezed the cup between his legs and sighed. 'I think I messed up badly.'

I thought about the letters he'd written and sent off. The sleepless nights. The bloodied hand. The newspaper scraps on the garage floor. The photo of the boy.

His chest was vibrating. I could hear my mother's footsteps, the clattering of dishes and the water running into the sink.

'Where did you go, when you went out?'

'I had things on my mind. I don't know how to explain. But they've gone, at last.'

Then I finally asked him: 'Have you ever been to the mine?'

He looked at me, once.

'Years ago. Why?'

'Just because.'

He shook his hands, as if trying to warm them, opened and closed his fists, brought the cup to his mouth and took a sip of coffee.

'You don't have to be scared,' he said. 'Everything's fine.'

'OK.'

'I love you.'

'Me too.'

'I love both of you. That's the truth.'

That day – Christmas Eve 1977, with the town in mourning, with not long left, though we didn't have a clue – I heard the springs creak from my parents' room, and my mother's muffled panting, their moans, then the door opening and him going into the bathroom.

You don't have to be scared.

I switched on my night lamp, got up, opened the desk drawer, took out the photo and a roll of tape, stuck it above my bed, switched off the light and fell back to sleep.

I.

I can only imagine those first moments.

She had missed the last bus and was walking on the edge of the road, the bag slamming against her side and her dirty T-shirt, a bruise on her right wrist and sore feet.

It was still warm.

She could've asked Ida for a lift but didn't: she was angry at Simona – over lunch she had squashed the food on the table, spilled fruit juice all over her, yanked her, screaming – and didn't want to see her again.

I have often wondered what she was thinking about. Maybe she was asking herself what someone like her was doing in a job like that, one that required infinite amounts of patience. A depressing place, in the middle of the woods. Maybe she just looked around her, the thorn bushes and criss-crossing trees, the restaurant on the day it's closed with its empty car park, the roof of a house further down the slope. I see her shaking her head – long, curly hair – looking at the stains on her white T-shirt, and sighing.

Suddenly, she notices the silence: nothing but the birds singing, the echo of her own shoes, the shadows settling in behind her. She rustles around in her bag looking for cigarettes, then remembers she had the last one while she was clearing the table.

She picks up a dry branch and whips the air. Mosquitoes and gnats.

After a bend in the road, she sees a white van approach.

She knows the driver, but at first he must look like a shadow behind the windscreen.

The van slows down, then stops.

Hello, she says.

The man leans out of the window and smiles at her. His hair is dusty, his shirtsleeves rolled up. His left hand taps against the van door, as if counting down the time.

Everything good?

I missed my bus.

That's a shame.

Yep, she answers.

My father looks at the road ahead, and into his wing mirror.

It's a long walk, to get home.

It's just that my feet hurt, she says.

Maybe she's about to say 'goodbye' and keep on walking. This is her last chance.

I'll give you a lift, he tells her. Come on, get in.

No, seriously, you don't have to.

It's no problem.

His smile is open and welcoming. It's quite the stroke of luck, really.

Really? Thank you.

She steps up to the van, throws away the stick, while my father, mouth dry, hands shaking, frees up the passenger seat – an electric torch, crumpled cigarette packets – throwing everything onto the floor.

She opens the door.

It's filthy, he says. I'm sorry.

No, it's fine, she says climbing in. Thanks again.

Not at all, it's a pleasure.

No one sees him drive over to the restaurant's car park, turn around, head back onto the road and drive away.

Anna

It was a dry, windy afternoon, after school had ended, when I saw a boy at the petrol station, sitting on the wall at the end of the forecourt . He waved in my direction, I waved back.

My father paid for the full tank, got back in the van and stopped for a second.

'Are we going?' I asked.

'I can't take you any more. I forgot I need to do something.'

We were heading over to where he worked – the small semi-detached-housing development. He'd been working there for three months, as a manual labourer. I was curious and had asked to visit.

'And what am I supposed to do?'

'Take the bus and go home.'

'Can't I go with you?'

My father just blinked. It would have been pointless to argue. I huffed and got out, and watched him head off in the dust; then I turned to the young man: he had stood up and was staring at me, rubbing the sole of his shoe on the tarmac. He came over towards me.

'Did he dump you here?' he asked.

'Looks like it.'

'That makes two of us.'

He was tall, skinny, black eyes that were too small for his face, long hair, red spots on his cheeks.

'I've not seen you around before,' I said.

'Got here two days ago.'

He nodded towards the house behind the petrol pumps, and towards Santo Trabuio standing in front of his shelter, in his blue jumpsuit, dirty cloth in his hand.

'He's my mother's father,' he said.

'You mean your granddad?'

'I don't even know him.'

It took me a second to realise what he meant – I knew about Trabuio's daughter, who had run away with a guy when she was really young, disappeared; I knew my mother didn't like her. At the funeral for Santo's wife, someone said: 'She should be ashamed. Didn't even come back for her mother,' and she added: 'What were you expecting? You know what she's like.'

'Are you here for the holidays?'

'This place? Are you a moron?'

'Oh OK,' I replied. 'Sorry.' I made to leave.

'I'm Stefano,' he said.

'Elia.'

He smacked his lips, and threw a sad look at the other

side of the road, a sea of grass whipped by the strong wind, then asked: 'Do you want a smoke?'

'Sure.'

'Come on, then.'

He headed off, hands in his pockets. I followed him across the tarmac.

This is another side of the story – my side.

When I saw her, in the small garden behind the house, next to a rusty car, hanging out the clothes, Anna Trabuio was humming.

I greeted her; she shielded her forehead and studied me.

She was wearing a sundress and leather sandals. Dyed hair – a pale blonde, washed out – thin lips, sunken cheeks, prominent cheekbones. She looked like she hadn't eaten in days. She was standing amid the weeds, the river at her back behind a wire fence and a couple of skeletal trees.

She said, 'Hi.'

She didn't ask who I was, then she leaned over and unravelled a towel from the laundry in her basket.

'Come on,' he said.

I followed him into the kitchen – the smell of burned food and dirty dishes – and down a hallway.

'Shut the door,' he said, stepping into his bedroom. He pulled a packet of MS out of his pocket, waited for me to take one, hopped onto the window ledge, flicked the lighter and took a drag, before handing it to me.

'Does your mother know you smoke?'

'Why? What's the problem?'

'Nothing,' I said.

The room was a dump, a pink throw on the bed and faded flowery wallpaper. On the desk, an open suitcase, a pile of clothes on the chair.

'Do you sleep here?'

'For now. It was my mother's room. We both stay here, there's another bed under that one.' He looked out at the road and the browning hills and the gathering clouds. 'Where were you going?'

I told him about the construction site and my father's job. 'What does yours do?'

'Stuff, in different places.'

'And where do you live?'

He used to live outside Turin, first floor of a block of flats, he said. There were a lot of kids in the area: he knew everyone. A field to play football, shops, warehouses. The kitchen windows shaking when trains went by. His parents had started arguing, he added, slamming doors and shouting, then his mother quickly packed their bags and they had left.

'She didn't tell him.'

'You mean your father doesn't know you're here?'

'He *didn't* know, but I called him.'

We threw the butts away. Stefano stretched his legs and looked at the tips of his shoes. 'I'm not staying anyway. He's coming to get me as soon as he can.'

His mother's footsteps got closer, up to the door, she knocked, and walked into the bedroom. 'I'm getting dinner ready,' she said, and looked at me. 'You can stay if you want.'

She caught me by surprise, as I was about to leave.

'Is that OK with you?' I asked, and Stefano nodded. 'Where's the phone? I need to tell my parents.'

He pointed at the road: 'They cut off his home one,' he said, referring to his grandfather. 'There's another in the shelter, but he doesn't let us use it.' He pulled a small pile of coins out of his pocket. 'I have plenty.'

I called from the phone box at the crossroads, under the darkening sky, the wind picking up, watching Stefano stamp on a patch of grass on the kerb, running his hand through his hair.

I let it ring for a while. I was about to hang up when I heard my mother's voice.

'What?' She sounded exhausted. She held the phone away from her mouth.

'It's me.'

'Is everything all right? Is your father there?'

'He left. I stayed here.'

'Where?'

'The petrol station. He said he'd forgotten something.'

My mother let out a long sigh.

'I've been invited to dinner.'

I hadn't been out to anyone else's since that winter, which had worried her, so she livened up for a second and sounded happy. 'Yes, of course. Who by?'

'Santo's grandson. He got here two days ago.'

She didn't reply straight away, then said, 'I heard.' There was a bitter note in her voice. 'How will you get back? I'm tired this evening.'

The last bus left Ponte at ten to seven. I had asked for a scooter several times, but they never agreed to buy me one. 'Dad?'

'He needs to be up early.'

'Hang on.' I covered the mouthpiece with my hand. I glanced at Stefano: he had crouched down, and was pulling at the grass now, as if it had become personal. I looked at Santo Trabuio, further away, closing up his shelter. 'He's giving me a lift,' I told her. I would walk home, I didn't care.

My mother hesitated – *the son of the woman who ran away from Ponte, the one she didn't like*: that's what I thought, and I was partially right. 'Elia, why—'

'I have to go now, bye.'

We headed back to Stefano's house.

Santo Trabuio was at the table. He was still wearing his jumpsuit from work. He nodded towards me, then picked up his napkin and stuffed it into his collar.

Anna pointed me to a chair. 'There's a storm coming,' she said.

Door and windows were open, and the kitchen was half in the dark. Pots and pans were piled up in the sink. Two daisies in a glass jar on the worktop. The empty washing-up bowl by the fridge.

She sat down and filled up our plates, spaghetti with tomato sauce, and watched me, as if curious about the way I held my fork or how I chewed.

'There's as much as you want,' she said, and silence fell for a while, just the clinking of cutlery against plates. The wind was lashing against the trees and the washing on the line, in that dried-up garden.

'So, how did you two meet?' Anna asked.

'I came with my father . . .'

Santo Trabuio aimed his dark, dry eyes at hers: 'He's Ettore Furenti's son.'

My father's name thundered in the half-light.

She rested her elbows on the table and touched her lips. 'Oh, that's what it is,' she said. 'Of course, you look just like him. What's your name? I haven't even asked you.'

I told her.

'What a lovely name.' She shivered, and rubbed her arms. 'How old are you?'

'Sixteen.'

'Really? Like him. I thought you'd be older.'

I don't think that was true: I still looked like a child.

She asked me about school – a polytechnic, in town, the same one my dad had gone to. She said Stefano had failed a year, but he was actually smart, he just needed to apply himself.

'I'm not going back to school, I told you,' he said. 'Dad says the same.'

She tied her hair back at the nape of her neck, pulling it behind her ears. 'We'll see.'

It had started raining, heavy, solitary drops, then a sudden wall of water. Lightning cut through the sky. She jumped up and ran to close the door and windows.

'When I was small I used to hide in the wardrobe or under the table whenever the storms came,' she said. 'Dad, you remember that?'

Santo didn't reply: he took a cigarette out of its packet, lit it, exhaled a white cloud towards the ceiling and left.

She watched him disappear into the hallway.

We finished our meal by talking about the boy.

'We saw it on TV,' she said. 'They still haven't found who did it, have they?'

I shook my head.

'That place,' said Stefano. 'Is it far?'

'Which one?'

'The one they found him in.'

'Not really, no.'

'I'd like to go.'

Anna frowned at him. 'You need to keep clear of it.'

I didn't say that one cold, crisp afternoon in February, I

had climbed up to the mine, crossed the tape, crouched down in the snow on that ledge, imagining the boy's naked body and a man with no face circling him.

The rain was crawling down the glass and it was dark.

'I should go,' I said. 'I'm on foot.'

She turned towards me, lips still pursed.

'No way. Especially not in this weather.' She stood up, went to the hallway. 'I'll give you a lift. Let me just get my umbrella.'

We were left alone for a second. Stefano grabbed his fork, pressed the prongs against the tablecloth.

'I can come get you tomorrow, if you want.'

'OK.'

Anna came back into the kitchen with a bag clutched to her chest and car keys in hand. 'Couldn't find it,' she said. 'I never find what I'm looking for. Nothing new.'

The cold, damp air embraced us. The crashing of rain, the washing line and the soaked laundry.

'It might be a good idea to run,' she said and started to laugh, her laughter mixed with the wind and the rain, and I followed her along the pavement around the house and across the clearing, between the puddles, past the shelter and under the metal canopy where Santo's car was parked.

She was still laughing as we got in. 'It looks like we just showered.'

'I'm sorry; you really didn't have to.'

'Why? It's fun.'

I rubbed my face with my wet T-shirt. She looked into the mirror, brushed her hair off her forehead and ran her fingers under her eyes.

'It's been a while since I drove,' she said, studying the gear stick, the tip of her tongue sticking out between her lips. 'He sold our car,' she sighed.

'Who?'

'Stefano's father.'

She shifted the seat forward and started the engine, switched on the headlights. She set off, the engine hiccupped, and she turned on the wipers. Under the rain, everything – the petrol pumps, the sign, the road, the unkempt field and the hills – was uncertain and out of focus.

'All right,' she muttered when I told her to turn right, and slowed down as soon as we got onto the road in the woods. She was driving really slowly.

'What does your father do?' she asked.

'Used to work at the cotton place. Now he's a construction worker.'

She must have known about the closure, I thought, because she just nodded. 'And how is he?'

'Very well, thank you.'

'I'm glad.' She seemed relieved. 'He was a great kid. Around your age, one summer, he helped out in the workshop.'

'I know.' I also knew that Santo had closed it down after his wife's death.

The rain began to ease off, and Anna slowed the wipers. 'It was hard for your father, when he was left alone.'

'He never talks to me about these things,' I said.

'Well, we all have secrets, right? Even you, I bet.'

A fragment of moon, pale and veiled, peeked out from behind the clouds. We passed the straight road where, two months later, my father would pick up the girl.

'It's nearly my birthday,' she said, quietly, almost as if letting me into a secret. 'Thirty-six. But I could be younger or older. It depends on the moment.'

We passed the windows of the restaurant, shadows sitting at the tables and cars parked outside. The road was empty. After the last bend, I spotted the light of the porch between the trees.

'We're here,' I said.

The headlights lit up the driveway and the postbox. The van was in the yard, next to the car. The lights were off – I thought they must be sleeping. From Ida's house we could hear a song by Battisti: music was the only thing that could placate Simona.

Anna stopped the car and turned to face me. 'Your mother,' she said. 'Her name's Marta, right?'

I nodded, and so did she.

'You look like her too. Here,' she touched my forehead. 'Same eyes. I knew her. I knew everyone. It feels like a century ago. Maybe it has been,' she sighed. 'Please say hi to them from me.'

She leaned her head against the seat, as if she needed to rest for a bit. 'I like this song,' she muttered.

I listened, without saying anything.

'Goodnight then, Elia Furenti.'

She was staring at the trees, the spot where the road yielded to a path, and she didn't say anything else when I said goodbye.

II.

It smells of sweat, even with the windows down. And there's a layer of dust on the dashboard, on the floor, on the seats.

In the compartment in the back, my dad has fitted a mattress – for naps during lunch breaks, he said. Around the mattress a cemetery of crumpled paper, pens, pencils, a couple of bags with empty cans. Things the girl hasn't seen: she hasn't turned round to look – why would she?

She stares at the road and the trees from the height of the van, as her hair wafts in front of her face, gets caught in her lips; she pulls it back, scrunching her nose.

It would've taken you a while, he says. On foot.

Ida came back late tonight. She had work to finish.

Time flies, he says.

There are blank spaces between the words he speaks, as if he is choosing them with care and doubting his ability to do so. He tightens his grip on the wheel, and the girl doesn't notice how badly his hands are shaking.

Do you want a cigarette? he asks her.

Yes, please. I finished mine, I need to buy more.

Not a problem, he says, and nods his head towards a packet on the dashboard. Get one for me too.

He slides the one she gives him between his lips, waits for the lighter, flicks it two or three times, the flame dies out, then he half closes his eyes and relaxes, taking a drag.

I needed that, he says.

She glances at the floor, the torch she just grazed with her foot: she moves it away. I'm sorry I'm making you late, she says.

The warm wind slips into the van and twists the smoke into complex shapes that break against the windscreen.

My father turns to look at her for a second. He smiles around the filter, with eyes that are liquid, almost see-through. He never takes out his cigarette.

I couldn't just leave you there. A young girl, all alone. What happened to your wrist?

A small accident, she replies.

Simona?

Yep.

The light slides slowly towards the summer sunset.

A girl alone isn't good, he says. With all the things you hear about nowadays.

He changes gear just before a bend, slows down, white cracked knuckles. The girl thinks she hears birdsong – a small mystery in between the trees.

It's better to be safe, he adds.

You're right, she says, and Giorgio Longhi comes back to her, found at the bottom of a slope – eight years old – and the fact that no one was ever caught for it, and that memory is a dangerous place she does not want to visit, not after a day like this. She chases away the thought and rests her elbow on the door, blowing her hair off her face. She lets the ash fall. Lets her fingers open in the warm, damp, heavy air. She sighs.

I'm dying today, she says.

Yes, says my father.

The Girl

The house, buried in darkness. The door wide open.

I stepped in, closing it behind me and locking it. I heard Anna's car leave and my mother whisper.

'Please,' she was saying, but I couldn't hear the rest.

After a second, she appeared in the hallway: her small frame. She came into the kitchen and switched on the light.

'Hello,' I said.

She stepped back, brought a hand to her neck and stared, eyes wide. 'Elia. What were you doing in the dark?'

'I just got back.'

The table was still laid out. Next to my father's dirty plate, an overflowing ashtray and a butt in the glass, an inch of murky water. The air was saturated with smoke.

She hugged herself, rubbed her shoulders, went to open the fridge and took out a bottle – home-made lemonade. She pulled out a chair and sat down.

'It stopped raining,' she said.

She was in her pyjamas. She was wearing her pink slippers, the stuffed ones that usually disappeared with the end of winter. On the left one, one day, my father had drawn a pair of eyes, a round nose and a curly tail. He had circled the table, grunting, as my mother chased him, trying to get it back, and I laughed like an idiot.

She took a sip of the lemonade straight from the bottle – she never did that – and put it back down on the table. 'So, everything OK?'

'Yeah, OK.'

'You're soaked. You'll catch something.'

Anna Trabuio says hi, I wanted to say, but it didn't seem like the best moment.

Something happened in her chest, a small hiccup, held back. 'Are you planning on going back there?'

I understood what she meant. 'I think so. Tomorrow.'

She closed her fingers around the damp neck of the bottle. 'I should've put more sugar. And what did you say his name is?'

I hadn't. 'Stefano.'

She repeated the name.

'He's my age.'

He's like me, I wanted to add, because that's the impression he gave me – sitting on the wall, alone, a single nod, *Do you want a smoke?*

'You should be going out with your friends,' she said. She drummed her fingers against the glass and frowned.

'You're better off not getting to know some people. Leave them be. I want you to keep that in mind. Go to bed now. Your father isn't at his best.'

She put the bottle back in the fridge.

'What's wrong with him?'

'He just needs to sleep.'

'But where did he go today? Did he say?'

She moved the chair back under the table and started tidying up.

She didn't tell me about the phone call she'd got. After he left me at the petrol station my father had called her from the *bar-tabacchi* along the road, telling her I was with him, sitting in the van, waiting for him, telling her he was feeling weird. I only found out about this months later. That summer, each of us kept something secret – just like Anna had said. My mother hoped that it would be enough to shut up, for as long as possible. I can't fault her for it.

I dried my hair with a towel, in the bathroom, looking in the mirror. My mother's forehead, that was it, and her chestnut eyes.

Back in my bedroom I undressed, opened the window slightly, and lay down on the sheet in just my underwear. The photo of the young boy. My mother's footsteps in the hallway, shortly after, and the creaking of the bed.

I pushed against the wall, turned on my side, thinking of Stefano coming towards me, from behind the petrol pumps, in the scorching heat of the afternoon. Before falling asleep, I saw my father's van, down the dusty road, I saw it turn and disappear over the horizon.

That morning the sunlight was sneaking through the blinds.

I could hear the water running in the tub, the metallic sounds of the plumbing, the birds singing.

I wondered if he had stayed home or already gone to work, and I remembered what he had asked me one evening, earlier in the week, sitting down on my bed, looking at his hands.

'I was thinking . . . There are people who always make it, in life, and others who just can't. Which do you think I am?'

'You make it,' I'd said, and he had hinted at a smile and pressed his fingers to his temples.

'I hope so.'

My mother left the bathroom and headed to the kitchen. I stood up, put on my jeans and joined her. She was standing in front of the window, in her robe, holding a small cup.

'Did you sleep well?' she asked.

I grabbed a bag of biscuits and sat down. 'Yeah. Dad?'

'He's at work.'

'Is he better?'

'Hm? Oh, yeah, it was nothing.' She sipped some of her

coffee. The light fell at an angle across her shoulders and hair. 'Everything is so slow today,' she said. 'Did you thank Santo Trabuio for the lift?'

She didn't wait for my answer. She went back to looking out of the window. 'How long are they staying, do you know?'

'He didn't say.'

She rinsed her cup. 'I'll go and get ready,' she said. Then she stopped, and cleared her throat: 'Leave him alone. That kid I mean. I'm sure he's like his mother. Some people just don't care about others. They don't care about how you feel.'

I wanted to ask her what she knew, and what that woman had done to her.

'Try not to forget that,' she added.

She went to get dressed, the hangers clinking inside the wardrobe. I ate a couple of biscuits. She came back into the kitchen with a sweater over her shoulders and her bag under her arm. She hadn't combed her hair or put on any make-up, and she seemed lost.

'I need to go now. Don't be annoyed at me for saying these things, I'm your mother.' She puckered up her pale lips, threw me a kiss and left.

I looked at the grass, still damp after the rain, the blinding light and the clear sky. The singing of birds filled the silence of that morning.

*   *   *

I waited for the bus under a tree, in the shade.

I'd already started walking when it arrived – the screeching of the brakes, the puffing of the doors as they opened, those few passengers who'd made it all the way up there – and I watched the girl step out onto the ground, yawning, her canvas bag, the dark mess of hair. She was wearing a light blue T-shirt, tight around her breasts.

'Oh, hey,' she said, and yawned again.

We bumped into each other on the street, sometimes, chatted a little, I asked her for cigarettes. She had worked for her mother for a year, at the haberdasher's, before she got fed up – 'we argued all the time' – and she had ended up with Simona: 'I can't really complain, but there are days when I want to run away.'

She was twenty-one that summer, and had an old boyfriend she was still fond of, I thought, though she spoke condescendingly of him – 'his loss, really'.

'Can I come with you?' she asked me, as I stepped onto the bus. 'No work today.'

She clapped her hands and pretended to burst into tears, as if desperate.

She wasn't a beauty – her legs were too thick, the skin on her face too shiny – but there had been a moment, the previous year, where I would've paid to kiss her or see her naked: I'd lock myself in the bathroom, imagining her, touching myself, trousers and pants round my ankles. One day, I'd seen her light herself a cigarette, on the other side of the low hedge, walk round the corner of the house – where was Simona? – pull off her top and sit down on a deckchair, in the sun, in her bra. That image stuck in my dreams, constantly, for months, with her calling me and unhooking her bra. Then it just went.

I hadn't told her, obviously. Nor had I told her I'd never had a girlfriend.

I gestured to her to come back onto the bus and she smiled.

'Maybe another time,' she said.

I sat at the back of the bus and turned round, and on the other side of the dusty window she raised her hand. I slowly moved my fingers, in response.

The image of her showing up in my dreams became like a rip I couldn't sew back together, when my father stopped, asked her where she was going and took her into the woods.

III.

August, night. The last one he spent at home.

I woke from a dream in which my mother stepped out of the van and asked me: 'Did you know?'

What? I wanted to ask her.

I kicked the sheets to the foot of the bed. I was thirsty – I was boiling and drenched in sweat – and went to the kitchen for a drink.

My father asked: 'Is that you?'

I stepped across the open doorway.

He barely turned his head. He was sitting with legs splayed, beer in his hand.

'What time is it?' I asked.

'The clock is right there, I believe.'

I'd found him on the stairs the previous week, wailing, hitting his head with his fists: 'I can't take this pain any more.'

'OK, I'll go back to bed.'

He mumbled something.

'What?'

'I said I can't breathe. It's like someone is suffocating me.'

'Is it the heat?'

He was wearing a pair of shorts, barefoot. He brought the can to his lips and took a long gulp. 'If only,' he said, and dried his lips. 'Is your mother asleep?'

'Yes.'

'Good. Better.' He put down the can. 'Do you see anything, over there?' he asked me, pointing out towards the road.

'No. Why?'

He shook his head. 'Doesn't matter.'

I went back to my room and looked up at the shadows on the ceiling.

I felt like I'd lived through that scene before.

January. It was dark outside, and it was snowing. I was reading my *Tex* comic, on my bed. My father walked past my room, hands crossed behind his head, and went into the kitchen.

'It's almost ready,' said my mother. 'Where on earth are you going?'

I heard a door slam. She called me. She was staring at the airing cupboard, arms hanging loose against her sides.

'Take him his coat,' she said.

'He could've got it himself.'

'Elia,' she turned towards me. 'Please.'

I put on my coat, grabbed his off the rack, and left. The air was freezing, the flakes thick and slow. I saw my father on the edge of the road, still.

'Dad,' I shouted.

He didn't turn, made no move.

'Dad?'

I swore and went towards him, snow against my face and in my collar. Once I got behind him, my father raised a hand.

'Look,' he said. He was staring at Ida's house, the lights in her lounge. The music was floating like snow. A figure was moving behind the glass: a swaying of the hips, clumsily, raising her arms and flapping them in the air.

'It's Ida,' I said.

Simona joined her, curved back, dangling head, hands on her ears.

I didn't like spying on them. I didn't like my father's expression, even if he said I shouldn't be scared. I handed him his coat but he didn't wear it.

'Are you blind?'

'Dad, I'm going back.'

As I walked away, he stammered: 'Can you really not see her?'

Honour Thy Father

I reached the petrol station.

Santo Trabuio was sitting in front of his shelter. I said hi, but he barely lifted his chin, looked at me, clicked his tongue as if I'd done something wrong.

'Did you take my car?' he asked. 'Last night?'

'Yes,' I replied. Had his daughter not told him?

He went back to staring at the wild grass.

I'd known him since forever. Someone just on the edge of my memories, since I was a child. My parents talked about him with affection, but I always found him impossible to read: especially after his wife's death. I'd never tried getting close to him.

'Bye,' I said, but maybe he didn't hear me.

I walked round the house and stopped in front of the kitchen, its open door. I peered into the half-light: leaning over the table, her back facing me, Anna was wiping down the Formica top. She put down the sponge and started scratching at the surface with her nails.

I cleared my throat and she turned her head. She looked at me for a second, then said: 'What are you doing, just standing there? Come in, sit down. Do you want a glass of water?'

'Please.'

She rinsed her hands, filled a glass and brought it to me. The water was warm, tasted of rust.

'Did you say hi to your parents from me?'

I said I had.

'Good.'

She looked at the morning light outside the door. 'Stefano and I had a fight. He went out. You can wait for him here, if you want.' She moved a chair and sat on it. 'Elia,' she said, as if my name had suddenly come back to her. 'It's just so weird.'

'What?'

'Everything.' She put a hand on the table and rested her head against her shoulder. 'I was trying to clean it. It's sticky.'

She stayed still, in silence. I wondered what she was thinking about.

At that moment, Stefano appeared at the door. She spun around, smiled and exclaimed: 'See who's here?' Her voice was warm and full of enthusiasm as she picked up my glass and moved it to the sink.

I said hi to him. He threw me a glare, touching his pocket that was bursting with coins, then turned to her and said: 'I did do it, you know.'

Anna sighed. 'Fine, whatever.' She took the dried-up daisies out of the jar and threw them in the bin.

We walked away under the silent stare of his grandfather.

We crossed the town square and walked onto the bridge. Stefano stopped for a second, leaned over the railing, and spat into the river. On the other bank, behind the furniture factory, the walls of the plant.

'My father used to work there,' I told him. 'Now it's shut.'

He looked up towards the chimneys, shielding his eyes, pulled out an MS packet and handed me one.

'Can I ask you something?' I said. We were walking along the road that led to the mine. The light was weaker between the trees. I picked up a stone and threw it.

'Shoot,' he said.

'What was it you did, earlier?'

'None of your fucking business,' he replied, and blew a ring of smoke. Then he added: 'I called my father.'

He didn't say what they'd talked about, or what he'd asked him – *So, when do you get here?* was what I imagined. *I can't stand it.*

That's how we became friends, that summer: between those silences, what we couldn't say and what we didn't get.

'Is that why you carry around those coins?'

'Yeah, the old man keeps them all in a box, in his room,'

he said. 'I took some, he'll never notice. And who gives a shit anyway?'

We were panting, between patches of shade and sunlight. He threw away the cigarette, stretched his arms and cleared the hair off his forehead.

'Did you know him?' he asked, suddenly.

'Who?'

'The boy.'

He had left his schoolmates and started walking – a woolly hat on his head, his schoolbag, a scarf around his neck. They had seen him at a traffic light, looking at the Christmas display in a shop window while waiting for the green. He crossed the road, then turned left, leaving the centre, on the road that bordered a field, an abandoned farmhouse, and a little further on, the fence of a tyre shop. Maybe three hundred metres. A car slows down – a man, no doubt about it – a door opening and an arm reaching out, a hand grabbing him. Or maybe he knew him and the man waves at him instead, asks him to get in, smiles, promises something – a sweet, a small gift. Nobody notices.

My mother had said that same evening, back from work, as she was taking off her coat in the hallway: 'They can't find a boy, they've been looking since this afternoon.'

I had followed her to the kitchen. She watched her reflection in the window.

'Who is it?' I asked.

'The son of the guy who owns the hardware store.'

I had seen him a couple of times behind the shop counter, and at the park, on the swings.

'I'll make food now,' she said. 'It's getting late.'

My father came home half an hour later – he'd gone who knows where. He locked himself in the bathroom. My mother went to call him, knocked, told him it was ready but he didn't reply.

When he came into the kitchen he sat down, only had a spoonful of soup, crossed his legs, and started smoking.

'Have you heard what's happened?' she asked.

He nodded, almost imperceptibly, staring at the wall, as my mother's voice crept around the silence – who told her, and where, and what did she think had happened? Nothing bad or irreparable. 'He must've been hiding and now he's scared, doesn't know what to do.'

'I'm going downstairs,' he added, and headed into the garage.

I only told Stefano part of the story: I didn't tell him about my father, the way he started staring at the wall. I didn't tell him about the photo I had stuck above my bed.

We left the woods, where the road flattened out again, and the sun shone on our heads.

'Who do you think it was?'

'How do I know?' I replied.

'There must be a lot of weirdoes out here,' he tapped his temple with a finger.

'It's the same everywhere.'

Everything up there was dried up, abandoned. A couple of low buildings were falling to pieces. Huts with caved-in roofs and missing doors, their walls covered in thick vegetation. Further up, the garage for the locomotive, with a rusty cart hanging out of it, tipped to one side. The entrances to the shafts, open and dark, and the tracks covered by weeds. We stayed there for a bit, looking around, smoking, then I pointed out the path that lost itself in a small wooded area.

'Nearly there,' I said.

We were almost out of breath, our T-shirts stuck to us, when we saw the tape between the trees, faded now, and I remembered that February afternoon – my footprints in the snow, the sky so blue and so far away.

'Over there,' I said, sitting on a log.

'You not coming?'

'Not now.'

'Why?' he asked.

'Because I've already seen it.'

Stefano shrugged. He headed off and stepped over the tape, leaning out to take a better look.

Whoever it had been, they had carried Giorgio Longhi to the bottom of the slope – the body was intact, no abrasions or fractures. A couple of metres away they'd found his shoes, without their laces, his folded clothes, his vest and pants, his socks, and the empty schoolbag.

'You know what I think?'

The air was damp, insects buzzing.

'No,' I replied.

He spat again. 'If they catch whoever did it, they need to kill them.'

I walked him home – Stefano asked me to.

We sat in the shade on the concrete step in front of the kitchen. I watched his mother take in the laundry. She was singing.

'Going for a piss,' he said.

She reached me with a full basket, brushing the grass into a cloud of dandelion seeds.

'You staying for lunch?' She had a film of sweat on her brow, a blade of grass stuck to her ankle.

'Maybe another time.'

She sucked in one cheek. 'That's a shame.'

She stepped inside, and we heard Stefano come back. He stood in front of me, hair wet, topless, shook his head and splashed me.

'Stop it,' I said, but he was laughing and I started laughing too.

'It'll cool you down.'

When I told him I was heading home, his mood darkened.

'You can call me though, if you want to do something. I'll leave you my number.'

He went back into the kitchen, opened drawers and cupboards and passed me a notepad and a pencil stub. I wrote down my number, tore off the paper, handed it over: he looked at it without seeing it, and pocketed it.

'Tomorrow?' I said.

'If I'm still here,' he replied.

Later, I found the van in the yard.

My father had glued newspapers to the windows of the back doors. A roll of tape had been left on the hood. I tried the doors, but he had locked them. I peered through the windscreen: in the dim light I saw the mattress.

'What are you after?'

My father had appeared on the porch. He was wearing his work clothes.

We looked at each other for a moment.

'I need to talk to you,' he said. 'Come inside.'

I stepped in and followed him to the bedroom. Blinds and windows were shut. There was a lit cigarette in the ashtray next to the bedside lamp: he lay down, his back to the headboard, and lit another one.

'You back already?' I asked. I had stopped at the door.

'Looks like it.'

'Why?'

'I had some things to sort out. Is your mother coming?'

'It's almost one o'clock.'

'We don't have too much time, then.'

He ran a hand through his hair, pulling it back.

'Do you know what one of the commandments says?'

I thought he was trying to make a joke. He didn't believe in God; he always told me: 'He was invented for the weak'. My mother was more open-minded, or maybe more insecure. We didn't go to church, other than for weddings and funerals.

'Which one?'

'Honour thy father,' he stuttered, and rubbed his face. 'Do you think there's anything to add?'

I thought about the van's windows. 'No.'

'Good. That's how it should be.'

He folded his legs then stretched them again, as if giving in to something.

'But it also says we must forgive. It's written, right? Somewhere, at least. So, I forgive you.'

I wanted to ask him what he was talking about, but I kept my mouth shut.

He looked at me from behind a cloud of smoke. 'Don't forget that,' he said. 'And the same goes for your mother.'

I waited for her on the porch, music in the air. She honked lightly when she saw me. She got out of the car, looked at the van, and asked me to help her with the shopping.

I went to fetch the bags and brought them into the kitchen.

'Is Dad already here?'

'Bedroom,' I replied.

She removed her watch, turned on the tap and rinsed her hands and wrists.

'He told me some things, earlier.'

She dried her hands and started rummaging in one of the bags. 'I'm sure I forgot to buy something, but I can't figure out what.' Is that how she felt, as her family fell apart? Then she looked at me: 'Did you go back this morning?'

'I'd promised,' I replied, curtly. 'Dad asked me if . . .'

She shook her head. 'Maybe you don't understand what I think of certain people. I haven't changed my mind.' She filled a pan with water and set it on the hob. 'Put the things away. I'll be back shortly.'

She went to him, the bedroom door opening and her voice: 'Darling, how are you feeling?'

I emptied the bags and went back into the yard, picked up the tape and took it into the garage.

My father didn't eat lunch.

'He fell asleep,' she said, draining the spaghetti. 'He had a bad headache. That's why he came back early.'

The air barely moved the curtains.

I divided the spaghetti into two twisted ranks. 'Do you want to know what he told me, or not?'

My mother chewed slowly. She pressed the napkin to her mouth and knotted her fingers, leaning her elbows on the table. 'Go on.'

She listened – honour thy father and all the rest – with her eyes half shut, as if the sun was shining right in front of her, then she started to smile. 'He was just talking. Don't think too much about it.'

I asked myself if she actually believed that, or if she was just trying really hard to convince herself that the worst was over by now. 'And what if it's like winter all over again?'

We had never talked about the letters again, of the days he'd spent God-knows-where, of the sleepless nights. The bloodied hand.

She straightened her back and cleared her throat. 'What on earth are you talking about?'

'Have you seen the van's windows? Did you see what he put in it? A mattress.'

'Don't worry, Elia. There's always a reason. Life is just complicated, that's all. And you can always choose, anyway.'

'Choose what?'

'To look forward or backwards.'

She picked up her fork and started eating again.

'Why don't you like Anna Trabuio?' I asked her.

'Did you meet her?'

'Well, yeah, she's there too.'

My mother looked at me, as if she expected me to insult her somehow – to share something unpleasant Anna had said or done – but I stayed silent.

'She thought she was *special*,' she said, then. 'She thought she was different. From me, undoubtedly. And she used to say as much to your father, too.' She tipped what was left on her plate back into the pan. 'Her parents were heartbroken when she ran away with that guy. But did she care? No.'

'She doesn't seem that bad to me.'

'Enough,' she said. She took off her apron, heated some coffee and poured it into a cup. 'I'll go and wake him up.'

She kissed me on the cheek and stroked my hair. 'Let's think about happier things.'

She loved both of us, and that was her life, the only one she had.

IV.

The girl sticks her arm out of the window, smelling the warm air.

At the end of the slope the light is still shining and Ponte catches fire, even if the ridge opposite is shrouded in shadows. The river is oil-coloured, a shimmering film on the surface.

She'll be home soon, she thinks. She lifts her feet up and frees her heels from her shoes, as the torch rolls around the floor.

Is that bothering you? my father asks. You can move it if you want.

Please, don't worry.

You're out of cigarettes, you said?

Yes.

We can stop for some if you want, I need to buy more, too. There's a tobacconist on the road that's still open, he says, as if she doesn't know, as if she doesn't live in Ponte.

Yes, that sounds good to me, thank you, she says, and he smiles again.

So the van takes the highway. Just a detour, a couple of minutes. There's almost no one around.

They'll wonder where we went, he says. Do you ever feel like running away?

Sometimes, she replies.

A gap in the bushes on the side of the road, where a steep path leads to the beach – that's what they call it, around there – a strip of soil and pebbles grabbed from the stream. There are bunches of houses in the fields. A scrapyard. The construction warehouse. Then the *bar-tabacchi*, a low building with rough concrete walls.

He doesn't slow down – he has started drumming his fingers on the wheel – then suddenly swerves. She clutches her bag, like a child in need of protecting.

Sorry. Did I scare you?

No, not at all, she replies, her voice shaking.

It's just that my mind's rushing. Too many things in it. I'll be more careful.

He stops the van next to the building, far from the entrance. Behind a wall there's a corn field, the last light over it yellow and dusty. Empty cardboard boxes, rubbish bins, a scooter.

Wait here, he says, taking out the key, clenching it in his fist. What type do you want?

I'll come, too.

I said wait for me.

Yours are fine, she says.

Perfect. So be it.

He turns, as he steps out of the van.

You can't leave, he says, showing her the keys – it's just a joke: why would she? – and she watches him disappear round the corner.

The owner was washing some coffee cups: he lifted his head as my father stepped in, and saw him glance back, before closing the door.

'No coffee,' he said. 'I just switched everything off.'

'Two cartons of MS.'

The man handed them over, took the money, gave him his change.

He was the last to hear my father's voice, that evening, other than the girl, and he talked about it to his customers the following morning, and with me, months later.

'His hands were shaking, I remember that. He looked back again, before he left, but there was no one there. I never saw any girl. How could I have known what he had in mind?'

An old colleague of his, shortly after, saw the van headed, lights out, towards Ponte, my father's face behind the windscreen – a matter of seconds – but nothing else.

'He looked alone to me,' he said.

I imagine my father in the car park, I imagine him getting into the van, giving her a lift – that's how I want to see – and coming home: still the man I know, or I thought I knew.

The Wall

The following morning Stefano called: 'Hey Tex, how are things?'

He came up with that nickname when I'd told him about my favourite comic and he said: 'Kids' stuff.'

'Good. You?'

I heard a car, next to the phone box, and the sound of brakes.

My mother was reading: she was headed to the library in the afternoon. My father was at work. He'd woken up earlier than usual and had gone, leaving her a note saying, *I didn't want to wake you.*

'Do you want to do something?'

'Like?' I asked.

'I dunno. I'm bored here.'

'OK, on my way.'

We said goodbye and hung up. My mother asked who it was.

'A classmate,' I said. 'I'm going out.'

I went back to my room to change. As I left, I poked my head in to say goodbye: she was lying on the sofa, feet on the armrest, in her pink slippers.

'Do you know what I'm reading?' She lifted up the book and showed me the cover: it was called *Wuthering Heights*. 'It's about not having what you want, and not wanting what you have. Or something like that. Not a nice thing.'

She was using my dad's note as a bookmark: it fell on the floor and she reached for it.

'Have fun,' she said. She added that she loved me and she hoped I did, too.

Anna Trabuio was stretched out on a sunbed, eyes closed. She was wearing her sundress; her shoulders were naked. Two long blue feathers at her earlobes. There was a bottle of soda with a straw in the grass. It looked like she was sleeping, but then she felt around the ground, found the bottle, brought it to her mouth and took a sip.

When she saw me, she said: 'Elia.' Those parted lips with which she spoke those syllables, and the air around her felt suddenly warmer and more dense. 'Is everything OK?'

'Yes, of course.'

I could hear the river on the other side of the fence.

'He's in his room, he's expecting you,' she said. She played with the straw. 'You're just like your father, so many years ago,' she added.

In the following months, I would imagine her in the summer breeze, bathed in sun, and dreamed of lying down next to her, suddenly waking up with her voice caught in my ears.

Stefano was biting his nails, seated on the floor by the foot of his bed.

'So, what do you want to do?' I asked.

'Let's go out.'

He took some money, his cigarettes and a lighter from one of his coat pockets, rolled up his sleeves. He didn't say goodbye to his mother; he didn't even look at her.

We played pinball in the room at the end of the bar, eyes fixed on the jittery ball. He bought two beers and we drank them in the playground where the previous summer I had seen Giorgio Longhi on the swings, hands tight on the chains, smiling. There was no one else there.

He put his bottle on the ground and grabbed onto the bar between the empty seats, folding his knees and hanging off one arm. 'Now what?' he asked.

We crossed the bridge and passed the furniture factory, stopping to look at the window displays, then reached the plant, its locked gate – over that winter, as he was writing his letters, my father had been convinced the padlock was part of the conspiracy.

Stefano tried pulling at the chain.

A stifling haze was covering the sun.

'We can get in,' I said.

'Really? How?'

'Come.'

He followed me along the wall, as I turned into the trees, until I reached a rusty barrel. I told him to climb on and he did, lifting himself up, bottle in hand, over the wall, then I did the same.

On the other side there was a pile of pallets. One brick building after another, writing on the walls, shattered windows.

'It looks smaller from the outside,' he commented, holding the half-empty bottle. 'What did your father do?'

'Repairs.'

I asked him again what his did.

'Nothing right now. But he always finds a way.'

'Is that why he argued with your mother?'

'None of your fucking business.'

We wandered around the different departments for a bit – bleaching and finish and weaving. The smell of urine and chemicals. Glass shards that reflected the light coming from outside.

He finished his beer and started hitting his leg with the empty bottle. 'Sometimes I just want to smash things,' he said. 'I was a troublemaker in school. That's why they failed me. You seem like a quiet one.'

I shook my head and took a drink of beer.

'Yeah, you are,' he insisted. He licked his lips. 'Someone who never reacts.'

'Only because you don't know me.'

He raised his eyebrows, flicked the lighter and looked at the flame. I wandered off for a bit. A piece of paper started floating, like a bird trying to take off. He joined me again, dragging his feet, and handed me the packet and lighter.

'Was that hurtful?'

'I just said you don't know me.'

'You don't know me either. Who cares?'

He chucked the bottle away. We walked into an office: two desks, upturned chairs on the filthy floor, a filing cabinet, folders on a shelf. I took one, smoking, and flipped through it. Stefano rapped his knuckles on the crumbling frame of a broken window.

'There's a cat,' he said, and clicked his tongue. 'Come here, kitty.'

I closed the folder and put it back, like someone would ever care to find it.

'You think your parents will get a divorce?' I asked. Other than Ida, I knew no one who had.

He touched his pocket, his coins, turned his head slightly, pulled up his T-shirt and dried his forehead. 'They're not married. She says she doesn't want him any more. But he can change her mind, you'll see. As soon as he gets here. Otherwise she's on her own. I'm not staying, that's for sure.' He looked out again. The cat was meowing.

'Shame,' I said.

'What?'

'If you leave.'

'Why? No friends, Tex?'

'I like being on my own.'

'Even better, then.'

We didn't say much as he walked me to the bus stop, but he waited with me and waved when I got in, and showed me his middle finger, smiling – squashed against the sky and getting further and further away.

Later, my mother's car came onto the driveway.

She stayed inside for a while, engine still running, and didn't notice me watching her, standing at the door. She finally got out, reached the grassy patch in the low, warm light, then opened her arms wide.

What was she thinking at that moment?

Her secrets and hopes and fears, the place where love held her tight: her open arms, no one she could hold or grab, the only thing she could do – and I walked away.

V.

So she's alone in the van.

As soon as he left, she took a look around her: she's seen the back windows, the newspapers and the dirty mattress, as if he slept there, as if he no longer had a home. Maybe he's argued with his wife? None of her business, either way. He gave her a lift, that's all that matters. She'd still be walking, exhausted, if he hadn't.

She hums a song, lowers the sunshade, cleans the dust off the small mirror, looks at herself. She purses her lips, drags her fingers around her nose. Her heart skips a beat when my father suddenly appears, leans towards the door and peers into the van.

She smiles and puts the sunshade back.

Are you making yourself pretty? he asks, licking his lips. Or were you nosying around? He turns towards the road, beyond the car park and the corner of the building, and finally gets back in. Here, he says, handing her a carton of MS.

Thank you, you shouldn't have.

We have a few each, this way.

He unwraps his and sets it on the dashboard, opens a packet and lights one. He rests his head against the seat. He seems tired or worried.

So, what were you up to?

Nothing, just waiting for you.

He looks at the corn field.

I didn't mean to keep you waiting, I met someone I know.

You were only a couple of minutes, she says.

Your parents must be expecting you.

The girl shrugs. They're not back till tomorrow.

And where are they then?

My mother's hometown.

The air smells of rust and exhaust fumes. The light is drying up. He closes his eyes, rubs his fingers on his trousers, hands shaking.

Is everything OK? she asks.

My head, I told you. It's like it's bursting.

He takes out the keys to the van, starts the engine and pulls out. They drive past the window of the *bar-tabacchi*, a final flash against the glass, and they take the road, a straight dark tape towards Ponte.

No one tells you, you know, he says.

What?

How people's minds work. The things inside.

He glances at the wing mirror.

You know what happened to me yesterday? he says.

No.

I was coming back from work, and everything went black. I found myself on the edge of the road, van sideways. Not like falling asleep. More like a light going out and back on.

The torch rolls on the floor and she moves it with her foot.

Don't worry, though. I could drive with my eyes shut.

Better not, she says, and he smiles.

It's just a joke.

He yawns. His elbow is against the window now.

Can I ask you something? How old are you?

Twenty-one.

Lucky you.

A car driving in the opposite direction flutters its headlights at them – someone he knows, maybe, a greeting. My father swears under his breath, throws out the cigarette and bites his lip.

Bad news, he says.

What do you mean?

That guy's following us.

She doesn't understand: for a second she thinks of the car that just passed them, the headlights flashing.

You see him, right? he says. What on earth does he want?

Before she can turn round, and before she realises, he changes gear. Turns onto a small road where the shadows become thicker, as the van drives off – no one can stop him – disappearing into the woods.

You Can't Leave

After his talk about forgiveness, my father seemed to find his good mood again. He'd sit on the porch, in the dark, he'd call me and make room for me.

'So, how are you? What are you up to these days?'

'I see my friends.'

I didn't tell him about Stefano and he didn't tell me about Anna, though I knew he must've known of her return to Ponte.

'And you're having fun?'

'Yeah.'

He'd rock the chair, nodding.

'Good,' he'd say, at my answers. 'Good good good.' He said that soon he'd take me to his work. He said it was a temporary gig, or so he hoped, there were better things in store for him. Watching the others work, he added, he felt 'a bit isolated'.

'But it's just me. They're all good people.'

He'd point his feet, pushing back again, and we'd swat the

mosquitoes or try to, slapping at our arms and neck. The music player, at Ida's, the music sliding over the porch. My mother would come to wish us goodnight, then she'd crouch and check the flowers in the pots, plucking out the dead ones – 'This summer is too hot' – and kiss him on the lips.

She was still wearing those pink slippers, as if part of her had got stuck in winter, my father's troubled days, or was waiting for more.

He'd tease her: 'Looks like it's about to snow, Marta. Do you need your coat too?'

On one of those evenings he grabbed her wrist and made her sit on his knees.

'You can't leave until I let you go.'

My mother burst out laughing.

And yet, something wasn't right.

He'd started parking his van on the road.

When my mother asked him why, he frowned as if confused by the question, shrugged and replied: 'To stretch my legs a bit.'

One day I peeked through one of the van's windows: I saw a torch on the floor, a roll of tape and a bag with a shirtsleeve poking out of it.

He started drinking a lot: I found a bunch of empty cans in the bin, next to the postbox.

I saw him in his bedroom, one Sunday, leaning with his forehead against their wardrobe.

'What are you doing?' I asked him.

He turned his head slightly and didn't answer.

In the stifling air, one evening, he asked me if I thought it was weird that I hung out with my father. He was smoking. He had a can between his knees.

'No,' I replied.

A chunk of ash fell on his vest but he didn't notice. He was staring at the shapes of the trees, at the end of the grass. My mother walked out, holding a jug, and started watering the flowers.

He said: 'They're dead.'

She turned and, as she saw the beer can, narrowed her eyes.

'Dead things stay dead,' he added.

My mother shook the jug, poured the remaining water into a pot, replied: 'Who knows. I'm going to bed,' and stepped back inside.

I made as if to get up, as if she'd asked me to follow her, but he grabbed my elbow.

'Sit,' he said. He finished his beer and asked: 'What do you think of your father?' He had asked me that once before.

All the time I spent next to him, he referred to himself as if he were someone else, someone not present, someone we knew but who had left however many years ago.

'What do you mean?'

'Do you think your father is a failure?'

'No.'

'Do you think he's worthless? The truth.' He put down the can, threw his head back and shut his eyes. 'You haven't thought about it, have you? Your father told you and you didn't think about it. He's the only one who can make decisions, you get that, don't you?' He stretched his arms and looked at his hands, rough and shaking.

'Can I go now?' I asked.

'I think so.'

So I stood up and walked towards the light.

In bed, later on, I heard his footsteps in the garage, his cough, something falling. I imagined him heavy and enormous, capable of taking over every inch of our house and the yard and the grass and the woods, slithering under the plants, the dry soil, the stones and the roots.

That morning, Ida and Simona walked down the driveway.

I was crouched in the shade, with a cigarette, and they didn't see me until I chucked it away and walked towards them.

Ida was holding a dish covered by a napkin. She said the girl was late and she needed to go to work, but she thought she'd pop in.

'Mum has already gone.'

'I know,' she replied, handing me the dish. 'Chocolate cake. I made it last night. All for you.'

'Thanks.'

Simona, behind her, mumbled my name.

'I hope it came out nice,' said Ida. She looked up at the sky and sighed. 'I was so hot last night that I wanted to sleep outside.' She waves her hands like a pair of fans. 'How are you?' she asked, suddenly.

'Good.'

'You sure?'

'Yes.'

She stood there for a second, then slapped me on the shoulder. 'Have a good day, Elia.'

VI.

What happened?

She has dropped her cigarette pack: she bends over to pick it up, feeling around on the floor, puts it in her bag.

Stay still, please, he says.

Why did you turn here? She reaches out with her arm, fingers touch the dashboard.

Didn't you hear what I said? Still.

What happened? she asks.

The road is bumpy and twists between the trees. A small yard, another. Her eyes slide to the windscreen, then stop on my father.

Everything's fine, he says. He must've got into his car as we were leaving the car park.

Who?

I didn't tell you earlier, but I was keeping an eye on him. He was drunk. He said he didn't like the way I was looking at him. I bought the cigarettes and left. I thought he'd give up.

The van carries on forward with no lights, rattling, in the middle of the lane.

Who is it? she asks, even though she's sure she hasn't seen a car. Maybe I know him. She thinks this might be important, a piece of the puzzle, but he doesn't reply. So she leans out of the window to check, pulling her hair back from her eyes.

There's no one there, she says.

He didn't turn off in time, he says. But he can come back, I don't trust him. You didn't see his face. He was looking for a fight and I don't fight with anyone.

Then silence falls. My father's hands clutching the wheel, the girl sitting still.

She must've believed it was true, initially: someone who'd been drinking and looking for a reason for a fight. But she thought it strange he hadn't just sped up, rather than turning onto this road, and hadn't stopped talking to her, especially that elbow resting on the window like that, as if it were nothing.

In a small clearing, an abandoned fridge on its side. A tyre. Rubbish bags.

There are crazy people out there, he says.

Are we going back now?

I'm thinking about it. Just give me a second.

She sees a light shining through the trees, behind a closed gate. She follows it with her eyes until she loses sight of it. There is a dog barking, in that yard.

I know this road, he says. I've been here before. There's a fork further ahead. I don't want to run into him again. Are you hungry? Thirsty?

She shakes her head, holding her bag tighter to her chest.

There's some stuff to eat in the back. And some beer. We could live it out for days. His voice is stable now, as if he has a plan in mind. He slips another cigarette between his lips.

You know, when I was small I had a dog, too. It was a beautiful thing. Always followed me, slept in my bed. Before I got up, it'd be there, wagging its tail, as if it could read my mind. Always looked like it wanted to tell me things. One day it disappeared and never came back. I looked for it everywhere, but it was dead when I found it. In the woods behind my house. They'd tied it to a tree and it choked itself from pulling at the rope.

Who? Why did they tie it up? she asks, though she doesn't really care right now.

Someone who wanted to have fun. Dickheads.

It's almost dark, now, and she looks around: trees and bushes. As they drive in silence, she thinks back to the car park.

I saw nothing. There was nothing there.

It's late, she says. I should be home. He slows down and stops at the side of the road.

I'm not doing this on purpose you know, he says. And it's not my fault.

I didn't mean that.

That guy is still out there.

Maybe he's gone.

He shakes his head. And there's no one home at your place, he says. We have all the time we need.

They head back onto the road. The wind slips in through the windows, smell of grass and rotten leaves. The torch rolls across the floor. Darkness rises from the ground, expands across the windscreen and attacks the sides.

Almost there, he says.

The fork?

Almost there.

He changes gears, takes a deep breath and smiles.

Laughter

One afternoon Stefano showed me a brooch.

We were sitting on the bonnet of the rusty old car, next to the washing line. We had no idea what to do.

'Do you think it's gold?'

'Looks like it,' I replied.

He brushed his hair off his eyes, the brooch shining in the palm of his hand.

'Where did you find it?'

He looked at me and grinned. 'I'm a lucky man, Tex.'

Whenever he was alone at home, he'd rummage through drawers and cupboards – later there would be a neck chain, then a pendant and a ring. He'd steal notes from his grandfather's wallet and his mother's purse.

He tucked the brooch back in his pocket, climbed off the bonnet and lay down in the grass a step away from the fence, an ankle resting on his knee and his eyes closed.

'And if they catch you?'

'You're a pain in the ass,' he said. 'But I will miss you.'

His father hadn't shown up yet. He called him often, but whenever I asked him what they'd talked about he always said: 'None of your fucking business.' There were days when he was distant, grumpy and aggravated – he'd argue with his mother, with me, about that 'shithole' where he'd ended up – and others when he was sad and defeated, just another spotty kid. Then there were days when everything went smoothly, and we had fun, and I thought he liked me.

I wondered what he was thinking about, or if he'd fallen asleep, when a window creaked, so I turned round and saw Anna, in the bathroom, hair bunched up in a towel and another around her chest. She leaned towards the mirror and undid the towel: her damp hair fell on her naked shoulders. She brought a hand to her face and touched her cheeks and eyes, her shoulders vibrating, and it looked like she was crying.

'What are you looking at?' he asked.

'Nothing.'

He'd sat up. He was silent, then frowned, staring at the window, then he suggested we go to my place.

'You've never taken me there,' he said.

'I'd rather not.'

'Why?'

I mimicked him: 'None of your fucking business.'

I didn't want to tell him about my mother – what she thought of his mother, the displeasure with which she'd told me not to waste my time. And the lies I told when I went out.

He crossed his legs, lifting his eyes to the sky.

'We can go swimming tomorrow if you want,' I said. 'There's a spot where we can dive into the water.'

'I don't have my swimming trunks.'

'I can lend you some.'

'I can't swim,' he said through clenched teeth, undoing and redoing his shoelaces, like he was embarrassed by the admission.

'I'll save you.'

'I'm screwed, then.'

He asked me to describe the place.

'You need to see it. It's just a bit far out. People usually just go to the beach, at the river.'

'Isn't it dangerous?'

'What, you scared?'

'Fuck off.'

He'd tell me that quite often, with his hard, worried stare.

'You first.'

'I'm fucked already.'

Storms that left as soon as they'd arrived.

I can't actually remember what we did that afternoon. Time came to meet us, and when we faced it, when we were together, it seemed to slow down, and that was enough.

I remember we laughed about something he'd told me – his hiccupping laughter, the way he squeezed his eyes – and that his mother came out and just stared at us. She ended up laughing, too, and I liked that image – the three of us laughing, in Santo Trabuio's poor excuse for a garden. I thought there could be nothing in the world to be afraid of.

My father didn't come back for dinner.

As I was waiting at the bus stop, I saw his van turn onto the bridge, towards the plant and the road heading up to the mine.

My mother put her napkin on her lap, glanced at her watch and turned to look at the dusking horizon.

I asked her if she was worried.

She smiled: 'It's not the first time, right?'

'So do something about it, then,' I said. 'He got that van and you said nothing. And he's always out when he wants. Doesn't it make you angry?'

'I trust your father.'

I shut up – she was still smiling – then I told her where I'd seen him that afternoon. 'What was he doing there?' I asked.

She narrowed her eyes slightly: 'What are you thinking?'

'Everyone went to look for that boy, except him.'

'What's that got to do with anything? And how do you know?'

'I asked him.'

'And what did he say?'

'He said he was on the lookout.'

'See?'

'He was talking about the plant, Mum. The letters. He shoved one of them in my face. He didn't go looking for him.'

My mother lost all colour in her cheeks, as if I'd slapped her, so I gave up. *You seem like a quiet one*, Stefano had said. I collapsed onto the table.

I heard her sigh. She brought her hands together, touching her lips with her fingers. 'I just want him to find me here,' she said. 'For him to know I'm here for him, whatever he does. You're only sixteen, Elia. One day you'll understand. That's it.'

We finished eating. She cleared the table, sat down again and looked me in the eyes. 'And anyway, isn't there something *you* should be telling me?'

I felt my cheeks catch fire. 'No.'

'Are you sure? I saw someone this morning.'

'Who?'

'You know who,' she replied. 'Your *friend's* mother. She was pretending to look for a book, even signed up for a card. "We always see your boy," she said. "Every day." She even asked after your father. I hope she knows her place.'

I thought about Anna, how she looked like she'd been crying, in the mirror.

'Why didn't you tell me?' she asked.

'Because I knew you wouldn't like it. Don't blame me.'

'I'm not blaming anyone. I *never* do. Anyway, it doesn't matter. You're stubborn. I'll have to get used to it.'

She looked just behind me and got up.

'I'm going to lie down for a bit. If you care.'

My father got back an hour later – she was fast asleep.

I was reading *Tex* by the pale bedside lamp and the open window. I heard the van get closer, the thud of its door, the footsteps up to the porch, where he stomped his shoes, the door opening, the keys on the table.

I went into the kitchen and found him sitting down.

He turned to look at me.

'Where did you go?' I asked.

His shirt was undone and he was drenched in sweat. He raised his hands, as if I'd threatened him and he wanted to surrender, then he fell back on the chair and burst out laughing.

'Well?' I went on. 'Tell me. I saw you today.'

His laughter stopped. 'Don't you dare.' He slammed his palm against the table, the keys shook. 'You saw nothing. Ever. Now leave.'

I went back to my room. I switched off the light, curled up in bed.

A couple of minutes later I heard a noise in the yard. I looked out of the window: my father in the middle of the grass, his shirt inflating and slapping against his back. He was smoking, the tip of his cigarette like a star he'd caught, brandishing it in his fist – like he held all of us. He started gesticulating.

It's not starting again, is it? I wanted to ask him. *You have nothing to do with what happened, right?*

He stepped away, cutting across the grass diagonally, fading into the darkness.

VII.

They keep driving with the headlights off.

So, where's this fork? she asks.

No idea, maybe we passed it.

I didn't see it.

I said maybe.

Should we go back?

He said he knew the road, not long ago, and now he seems to be lost, not sure of where they are, at least. Let's keep going, he says.

But there's nothing here.

It's what I wanted.

My father rubs his thumbs against the wheel, arms tense and jaw stiff. She looks at the wing mirror: just a wall of trees in the dark.

I need to keep my lights off, he says.

Why?

Stupid fucking question.

The smell of soil and air, the first stars pulsing in the sky.

I'm sorry, I didn't mean it, he says, I don't mean to be rude. You'll see, he'll go away, I was thinking.

He wears down his words: keeps them in his mouth for too long and then spits them out, stumbling.

We just need to go back, she insists.

True. But it's not that bad, really.

What?

This, here, he replies.

She thinks of the mattress, in the back of the van. Then of his wife. His son, as he asks: Do you have a cigarette? Their images flicker in the dark and disappear.

Maybe you got it wrong, she says.

Got what wrong?

The road isn't this one, maybe.

Who knows, he says, again.

She tightens her grip on the door handle. She's sure of it now: no one has followed them. She could tell him to stop, she could ask him to let her out, but she has no idea where they are.

I've never been in a fight, he says, pulling out another cigarette from the packet. I'm not that kind of person.

His hand is shaking so badly he has difficulty bringing it to his mouth. He slows down, taking a drag. They kicked me out and I had to say it. I said everything. Do you want to know what I think? I think they did it on purpose. They did it. They sent him, that guy.

The shapes of the trees in the clear sky. A branch

scratches against the van and the girl recoils – *Don't answer him*, she tells herself, *don't ask anything else*.

I was the lookout, you know? I saw them go in and out every day, he says, and fit the padlock and chains. I wrote about that, too.

He narrows his eyes and turns towards her. Are you listening to me? He turns back to look ahead, lifts his hands off the wheel and they start veering left, towards the trees, and she screams: Watch out!

He brings them back onto the lane. Laughs. I thought you were asleep.

No.

Because I'm awake.

She can't breathe. She can't swallow – her mouth full of saliva. *You need to calm down.*

We'll stop soon, he says. Hide for a bit. So he can't find us. Then I'll take you home. Isn't that a good idea?

She stays silent.

I asked you a question. Hello?

Where are we stopping?

Never answer a question with another question. It pisses me off.

All right.

I can't be pissed off right now. You don't need it either.

A short straight lane, a patch of woods that seems to close in, further ahead. Impossible to see beyond it.

Think about it, he says. If he took this road we'll have him behind us any second now. And there is no one else but me.

My father breathes deeply and puffs out his chest, then throws out the cigarette, smoke pouring out of his nostrils. He slows down, changes gear and they turn onto a path: a bundle of trees, stones under the chassis and branches against the windscreen, darkness, and everything she knew, or thought she knew, suddenly disappears behind her.

Falls

I woke up before lunch, the sun flooding my room, the house quiet.

I made myself a sandwich, washed, put my trunks on under my jeans, grabbed another pair and stuffed them in my pocket.

I was choosing a T-shirt when my mother got home. I went into the kitchen and found her in front of the fridge.

'I'll make some food now,' she said.

'I already had some. I was hungry.'

She took something from a shelf, looked at it, and put it back. 'You didn't want to get up this morning.'

'I didn't hear you,' I said. It was true.

'Are you annoyed at me?'

'About what?'

'What I told you last night. Anna Trabuio and the other things.'

I said I wasn't – what was the point? 'I'm going into town.'

She closed the fridge and stared at me. 'I gathered,' she said.

I didn't tell her what we had planned.

We called them the falls. We all knew that stream, but no one but me ever went there. The beach was closer, and the others preferred to lie on the pebbles, on their towels, and the water there was warmer. She didn't like that place: 'Don't go there again. Your father had an accident once,' she told me one day. 'I can't remember,' he replied, when I asked him what had happened.

'I'll eat by myself then. See you later.' She turned her back on me.

Sometimes I feel I should've told her about my father – in the grass, that night, gesticulating and walking off, and what I feared about that boy, and tried keeping out of my mind – but what would she say, my mother, the woman who loved us? What would she do?

I'd tried, and it had been pointless.

I knew nothing, back then, of the ways in which love can show itself, of the force with which it can push us into a corner and take our breath away.

I waved goodbye, walked down the driveway and stopped on the edge of the road, watching the girl on the other side of the hedge: she was shaking a tablecloth and talking to Simona.

She waved at me and smiled.

*　　*　　*

Stefano was sitting on the wall, waiting, biting his nails.

'I don't have towels,' I said. 'Should we go to your place to get some?'

'We'll make do. I don't want to see her.'

'What happened?'

He said he'd had a fight with his mother – for a change.

Santo Trabuio was washing a windscreen but aimed his gaze at him, as he stood up and patted the dust out of his jeans.

'He's watching you,' I said.

'So what.'

I wondered if he'd noticed – the missing money, his wife's jewellery – and what he was thinking, what he thought of this stranger who was his grandson.

'Come on,' he said. 'Let's get out of here.'

It took us almost an hour, along a steep paved road then along a path coasting the stream. The final stretch was even steeper, between creaking branches and dry leaves. The sound of rushing water. Then I saw the rocks through the trees, at the point where the path led away from the stream, headed who knew where. There was a natural pool, froth floating like mist over a field.

'Here we go,' I said. 'We need to climb down there.' We grabbed onto a tree trunk, feet sideways. He slipped anyway. On the pool's edge – soil and stones – he rubbed his hands on his butt and narrowed his eyes, staring at the rocks, the shimmering water.

'Fucking hell,' he said. He looked serious and focused, sweat dripping from his brow.

'Do you want to try or not?' I asked.

He nodded.

'Here you go then.' I chucked him the trunks and he caught them.

The side of the pool was in the shade: I shivered, removing my shoes, socks, jeans and T-shirt, resting everything on a fallen tree, then I turned the other way as he took off his pants.

'Don't you want to see my willy?'

'You're so gay,' I said, and Stefano laughed.

When I looked at him again, arms tight around his chest, he was staring deep into the water, trying to measure it. I thought about my father's accident.

'Don't do it if you're not sure.'

'Fuck off,' he said. 'Even if I drown who cares?' He slapped his hands on his thighs, stepped in front of me and started climbing.

'It's slippery.'

'Stop being a pain in the ass,' he shouted back.

When he reached the top of the falls and put his feet in the water, he shouted again: 'It's cold.' He just stood there, arms open like wings, balancing, staring at the point where the stream fell into the pool.

'Jump, I'm here,' I told him, and he let himself fall, hands fluttering in the air and the light, disappearing under the surface then coming back, his eyes seeking me out, arms floundering.

I got in up to my knees, holding on to the tree. The water was freezing. I reached out a hand to help him out of the water and he coughed and spat, then threw himself down by the tree. I said: 'Cool, right?'

Stefano nodded, catching his breath. 'Your turn.'

I climbed up, shouted: 'Watch this!' I jumped in with my knees tucked into my chest.

We kept going for a while, the sun warming us as we reached the top, on the rocks, until we were exhausted.

'Enough,' he said.

'I'm doing one more,' I said.

Before I dived in I thought about Anna: she emerged all of a sudden from a place I thought no one could reach, inside of me. I imagined her sitting in her son's place, wrapped in a towel, her hair dripping water. I closed my eyes and let myself fall.

Wet and shuddering, we rubbed our arms and legs, blue lips, teeth chattering.

'Cigarette?'

'Yes sir,' I replied.

He pulled out the packet and handed me one. We had no idea what time it was but the light had changed. We were good, there, alone.

'Can I ask you something?' I asked. 'You were pissing yourself, weren't you?'

Stefano pulled a face and frowned.

'Come on, it was obvious.'

'Shut up,' he said, and scowled at me. He looked disgusted. 'I'm never afraid.'

'Me neither,' I said.

He kept staring at me then shook his head.

I rested against the tree and looked up, the frothy trail of a plane. He said something I didn't catch. 'What?'

'I said I want to go.'

'Yeah, sure. Just a second.'

He chucked his cigarette butt away, picked up a stone and threw it into the pool, chin on his knobbly knees.

'What's up?' I asked.

'You all think you know what I'm like.' He threw another, and another. 'She's always saying that.'

'She?'

'My mother. "I know what you're thinking. I know how you feel." She says he doesn't care about us.'

His father must've popped back into his head, or maybe he just thought about him all the time – a skinny, tall man, that was how I imagined him, a shadow showing up in the paved area behind the petrol pumps, then the small garden and the concrete step: *I've come to take you home*, his hand on his son's shoulder, and Anna following them and I'd never see them again.

'She doesn't want me to call him. She says it's better for me. It's a bunch of shit, Tex.'

'But he hasn't come,' I said. 'It's been over a month.'

'He doesn't have a car.'

'Neither did you.'

I realised I shouldn't insist, because he looked at me like he was going to hit me then jumped to his feet.

'You live at home, so leave me alone.'

He reached the edge of the pool, pulled down his shorts and widened his legs for a piss.

We got dressed again and headed back on the path.

For a good while Stefano stayed behind, then I heard his steps quicken and I turned around.

He stopped, brushed his hair from his forehead. 'Things are just shit,' he said. 'Sorry.'

'OK.'

'Can we come back another day?'

'If you stop being a dick.'

'And if you stop pissing me off,' he said.

Head hanging down, he drew a groove in the ground with his shoe, as if trying to add something up, then he lurched forward, shoving me as he passed: 'You're too slow, catch up.'

I watched him getting further away. 'Wait.' I started running too.

VIII.

He drives the van to the end of the path then turns off the engine. He half closes his eyes in that new darkness, stretches his arm through the window, reaches out his fingers and closes his fist.

His name is Ettore Furenti and he is my father.

The girl – her name still rings out in my dreams, and it forces me to stop doing whatever I'm doing, caught by sudden terror, when I hear it in the streets, in a shop or in a car park, and I think it's her, that she's recognised me, thirty years later, that she's reappeared from the past and that she's looking at me, a name I cannot pronounce or even spell out, and which I saw written down in the *Eco della Valle*, next to my father's name, and on the silent lips of the people – the girl doesn't move a muscle, doesn't open the door, doesn't try to run away: she looks at the half-moon of trees tightening around her.

We're here, he says, and she turns around, almost

hoping not to see him again, just an empty seat instead of my father.

What are we doing here?

I told you already.

I want to go home.

Not now.

Why not?

He lights himself a cigarette and offers her the packet.

Go on, take one.

She shakes her head.

Don't make me insist, it's not polite.

He shoves the packet under her nose and she takes one and he passes her the lighter.

That's better. Good.

The girl's face, from what he can see – the flame lighting her up – is just a pale mix of shadows. She's weak and confused. The lighter falls from her hands – she can't hold it – then she looks up and apologises.

I'll do it, he says, but you stop staring at me.

He bends over and picks it up, puts it back in his pocket and rubs his eyes. His hands have stopped shaking now.

It's just that I can't sleep any more, he says.

He remembers the woods behind his house. The image of him digging a hole in the ground, his dog's gaping mouth, tongue lolling, but he can't remember when it happened. When did he bury it?

That's why I can't remember, he says.

Some things vanish into nothing, no matter how hard he holds on to them. Others survive, but he couldn't tell when they actually happened. Time has all bunched up like a bedsheet: sometimes he thinks he got fired the day before, or it's still winter and he's confused by the long, hot days. Then there are things he's afraid he's done.

It wasn't me, he says.

He leans his forehead on the wheel to rest, and at that moment he feels a movement, the click of the handle and the door opening.

What are you doing? he asks through his teeth.

Nothing.

Shut it.

She obeys.

Then he's back in winter again, it's snowing, it's dark.

He's on the edge of the road, at the top of his drive, Ida's house fully lit up, and the girl appears behind a window: she's moving her arms and twirling in on herself, her hair showering her shoulders. She dances for him, because she saw him, without his coat, in the cold – she likes him watching her. She calls him and her warm voice asks him to join her.

I'm waiting.

I wanted to come in, he says. But my son was there, I couldn't. But it doesn't matter now. What matters is that the guy doesn't find us. And that we stay together.

He takes a last drag. The wind is like a call.

Now look at me, he says, but she keeps her head low, her hand abandoned on her bag, cigarette burning away in her fingers. She parts her lips, murmurs: *Please*.

Let's get out.

Why?

We need to go.

Please.

We have to. We both knew we'd have to.

She doesn't move, so he sighs and gets out of the van, walks round the bonnet, opens her door, removes the cigarette from her fingers and takes a step back.

Come.

She shakes her head.

Come on. It's not that far. He takes her by the elbow, pulls her gently – what's left of the person he remembers, the night she danced? – and she moves her legs and gets out but can't stand straight, she's like an empty sack.

I've got you, he says. Now give me that bag.

No.

I said give it to me, there's a good girl.

He slides it under the seat, takes the torch, switches it on and shines it in her face. Her head jerks sideways, the girl moans and shuts her eyes.

Sorry, he says.

He lights up the weeds and tree trunks, a gap in the trees, asks her to look.

*   *   *

He left the van where it was impossible to see from the road.

He didn't shut the doors: the key was still in the ignition.

He probably thought it would take them days to find him.

He'd been there before, when he came home late with filthy shoes and trousers, or when he left after dinner and we waited for him.

To the plant, and along that path.

He knew where to go.

The Birthday

One Sunday in July, a man walking his dog along the river-bank found the boy's notebooks wrapped in a cloth. He handed them over to the *carabinieri* and was held for questioning, but on the day of the disappearance he'd been working, he claimed – the furniture factory. After work he'd gone straight home, he and his wife had dinner and went straight to bed.

His colleagues confirmed his version. His wife confirmed it.

Ida had seen him in the store, around lunchtime – I heard her talking about it with my mother – and they'd had a chat.

'Maybe it was still him, though,' said Stefano.

'So how'd he do it, then?'

'I dunno. They need to find out.'

'He wouldn't have gone to the *carabinieri* though.'

'Someone like that isn't right in the head,' he said.

'I don't think it's someone from around here.'

'So he went back? Just to plant the stuff?'

'Might have.'

'Oh, come on.'

The following week Anna turned thirty-six and she invited me to stay for dinner because, she said, she wanted to celebrate.

'I'll take you home, I remember the way.' She was beating egg whites. Standing barefoot, in the weeds. She stopped for a second, lifting the fork. 'But only if it's not an issue for you.'

'No, no problem.'

'You sure?' She was about to add something but didn't.

'Of course.'

'But you need to tell your parents.'

I said they weren't at home – my mother would only have complained and I didn't want to hear it.

'OK, then,' she said, and smiled.

'What is there to celebrate?' asked Stefano. He was sitting on the edge of the sunbed: he ripped a dandelion out, waved it in the wind, chucked it behind him.

'There's always something, sweetheart. Always.'

I imagined my mother waiting for me, worried – waiting for my father, too, maybe – then I erased that thought, as I watched Anna cross the grass singing under her breath, hair gathered on the nape of her neck, a veil of sweat beneath it.

* * *

The dinner was a disaster.

Santo Trabuio said nothing: he had a bite to eat, smoked a cigarette then left. 'I'm going to bed.'

'I made a cake,' she said, but got no reply.

There was some wine in a jug. When her father left – we heard the door slam at the end of the hallway – Anna poured some for herself.

'Don't you get it?' said Stefano. 'He doesn't like having us hanging around the place.'

'Being obnoxious won't get you anywhere, you know. And it's not true anyway.' She twisted a lock of hair around a finger. The warm air, the darkening sky. 'Can I ask what's wrong?' she said. She emptied the glass and filled it up to the brim again. 'I am your mother, after all.'

'I want to go home.' He kept saying that, all the time.

'For the time being, *this* is our home,' she said, with a tepid smile. 'You know what happened.'

'What?'

'Stop it.'

'You know no one can stand you, *Mum*.' She opened her mouth and started blinking.

I lowered my head, hoping it'd be over, that he'd give up. She touched his hand, lightly. Stefano growled: 'Don't touch me.' Then he raised his hand and hit her.

Anna fell back, stunned, kneading her shoulder, then she burst out laughing and drank some more wine. 'No one can stand me. It's true.'

Stefano stormed off to his room without even saying anything to me.

She murmured: 'No one.' She scratched her face.

'That's not true, believe me,' I said.

She looked at me. Her eyes were tearing up. 'How do you know?' She took the glass, brought it up to her lips. 'I'll take you home,' she said, 'You didn't miss out on anything.'

We left the petrol station under the streetlamps and moved off into the darkness. Small bunches of stars were pulsing in the sky.

Anna was letting the engine rev a bit too much, as if focusing on something she'd just remembered. 'I think I'm a bit drunk,' she said. 'I don't usually drink, you know?'

The only thing I knew was that I was sixteen and I was sitting next to the woman I lately hadn't stopped thinking about.

'You have no idea how it feels.'

'What?' I asked.

She thought about it for a second.

'To be alone. I'm sure you never will.'

I stuck a hand out of the window, stroking the warm air.

'Stefano told me you went to the falls,' she said.

'Yes, once.'

'But he can't swim.'

'It's not dangerous. I was there.'

'Did your father never tell you?'

'What?'

'What happened to him there.'

'No, he didn't. My mother said he had an accident. I think he fell.'

'He *fell*,' she repeated, and her tongue wandered in her mouth. 'She wasn't there that day. Just me.'

My father and Anna at the falls: what were they doing alone?

'What happened then?'

'Oh, never mind,' she replied. 'It was so long ago.'

The moon appeared above the trees, looking like a broken plate. Anna sped up just before a bend, and she had to brake suddenly to slow down.

'I really did have too much.' She laughed, pulled her hair back and looked at me. 'I imagine you and Stefano tell each other everything. You're always together.'

'More or less.'

'And did he tell you about his father?'

'A bit.'

She nodded. 'Let me guess: he said he hates me because I dragged him here. That it's all my fault.'

I hesitated, then said: 'No.'

'Of course he did.'

'He didn't, I swear.'

She massaged her temple and sped up again. We passed

the restaurant, its lit-up windows. 'So you're a liar like the rest of them,' she said.

At that moment a shadow appeared from the woods, stopping in the light – a cat, I think – only to disappear quickly over to the other side of the road. She slammed on the brakes, letting the clutch go. The engine stalled. I was jerked forwards, I planted my hands on the dashboard then fell back onto the seat.

'I almost hit it,' she said. She was panting. She stroked my shoulder. 'Everything OK?'

'Yes.'

She started the car again and drove a couple of metres, then pulled over and started sobbing, pressing a hand to her mouth.

'Are you hurt?' I asked.

She shook her head and straightened up. Then she turned to look at me, cheeks streaked with mascara: she dried them and tried smiling at me, as the sobs died down.

'I got scared,' she said, sniffing loudly.

'Nothing happened.'

'It's not been a great day. I didn't mean to grill you, sorry. You're so nice.'

I shrugged.

'It's true. Do you have a girlfriend?' she asked.

'No.'

'But you definitely like someone.'

I lowered my eyes to the hem of her dress, just above her knees. I suddenly felt like I was on fire.

'And do you like me?'

'Yes.'

'How much?'

I took a deep breath. 'A lot.'

She said again: 'Liar.' Then she rested a hand on my leg and squeezed it. I turned towards the light, the headlights still on.

'Look at me.' She came closer, took my chin between her fingers: 'Elia Furenti,' she said, and pressed her lips against my cheek.

I could smell her perfume, the scent of her hair, I felt my groin pulsating, my hands cold and damp.

She pulled back and burst out laughing, almost crying. 'Oh God, I'm such an idiot. I wanted . . .'

'I'm OK with it,' I murmured, and Anna narrowed her eyes, as if missing the implication of what I'd just said.

'Let's go now.'

That was when – as she gripped the wheel again without actually moving – that was when I touched her arm, her sweaty skin, then I stroked her. She didn't move initially. She just shivered. 'I'm not used to this sort of thing any more,' she said. I leaned over and kissed her, lips closed, and she let me.

Then she moved away and studied me, in the darkness. 'I need to take you home.'

'I don't want to.'

'Where do you want to go? Stay here?'

'I'd like that.'

She pulled her lips into a drained smile. 'That's an idea.' She threw her head back, her slim neck tracing an arc, took a deep breath and closed her eyes. 'I just keep running away . . . don't be like me,' she said.

Then we looked at each other, she sucked her lips and we kissed again – the wine on her breath – tongue tips touching, rubbing each other's arms, running our hands through each other's hair, almost like sinking together, entwined, unable to breathe.

All of a sudden she froze, hands tight on my shoulders, and turned towards the back window. 'I heard something,' she said, faintly.

'There's no one there.'

'Listen.'

We looked around, the empty road. She pulled her dress back over her legs and wiped her mouth.

All I wanted to do was start again, whatever it was, and keep doing it, kissing her and touching her, but she turned the key and started the car.

'It's late,' she said, and we set off.

She was thinking of her son, I thought later, even after all he'd said and done that evening. He would've asked her what took her so long.

Where the fuck were you?

I didn't care: there was only her mouth, her smell, my sore legs and my pulsating groin, right then.

She stopped the car far from the driveway, switched off the headlights, rested her back against the door and looked at me. 'It looks like you were in a fight,' she said.

I sorted out my hair and unstuck my T-shirt.

'There, that's better.' She closed her eyes and added a sentence I didn't understand back then. 'At a certain point, it's more the things you don't know than the ones you thought you knew. In the end, you realise you knew nothing at all.'

She stayed there, eyes closed, then looked at me again. 'Your parents are back,' she said, pointing to the car in the yard. 'You need to go.'

There was a tinge of impatience in her voice, something sour and rough I hadn't heard before.

'Happy birthday, then.'

She frowned.

'It is your birthday.'

'Yeah. You're right. Thanks.'

I was about to leave, but she said: 'Wait.' She moved closer and we kissed again, for a while.

When she'd disappeared down the road, I stared at the darkness she had left behind, touching my mouth, trying to slow down my heart.

The breeze was blowing through the leaves. Everything seemed small and far away.

I walked uncertainly down the drive – no sign of the van – breathing deeply as I stood on the porch for just long enough to regain my bearings, and stepped inside. The light was on in the hall.

'Elia, is that you?' my mother asked. She was in the lounge, in the dim light, sitting on the sofa.

'Where on earth were you?'

I stayed at the door, hands in my pockets, legs shaking.

'I missed the bus,' I said.

My mother tilted her head to one side. She didn't ask any more questions – I wondered if, looking at me, she'd noticed something.

'Where's Dad?'

'I don't know,' she replied. 'I was just thinking—'

On the floor, her slippers and an open book. She was wearing a pair of my father's socks.

'Want me to turn off the light?' I asked.

'Yes, please.'

I went to the bathroom, then to my room, closed the door and threw myself onto the bed. I fell asleep fully clothed – I didn't hear him come back – and that night I dreamed of Anna: lying on the back seat of the car, a place I couldn't recognise, on a clean, clear day.

IX.

The light from the torch gives life to the trees again.

Come on, he says. He opens the back door and goes in and out. Now he's behind her.

The girl's breath is fast and broken, as if she's been running on that hot summer night.

You said you were taking me home, she says.

Exactly. That's where we're going.

Before dinner, lying upside down on my bed, I was observing the sky getting darker, thinking of how, that morning, Anna had looked around, dragged me next to the fridge, took my hand and pressed it to her lips, rubbed it along her neck, as her son finished getting ready. We didn't speak.

My mother went into the lounge. She switched on the TV, switched it off again and went back into the kitchen. She was waiting for my dad to come home. Despite not talking about him any more, we both knew something was wrong: he slept very little and always on the sofa, he'd lost too much weight, drank too much, smoked continuously.

I undid my jeans and started touching myself. I imagined what Anna and I could do together, and where: in the car, at the falls, on the pebbles of the beach or in the *Futura* cinema hall.

My father was just a shadow, at that moment, just a thought I had stifled. There were days, back then, where I even hoped he wouldn't come back, that he'd decided to disappear, the house finally calm and quiet, and the echo of his footsteps nothing but a memory, his rough laughter slowly fading.

I heard my mother's voice: 'Elia?'

I did my jeans up, went to the bathroom to rinse my face, washed my hands.

She smiled at me when I walked into the kitchen. 'Nothing new,' she said. She pointed at my father's empty spot, as if his absence was just a detail, a stain we could wipe out, something she'd got used to, even though I knew that wasn't the case.

Where is he taking you?

He's taken something out of the van, he stashes it in his pocket. He lights up the gap in the trees, he knows exactly where they're going, as he repeats: 'Come on.'

Her legs collapse again and he has to hold her up.

Don't be afraid, he says, torch aimed at her feet. Come on.

She murmurs: I can't.

I can't hear you if you speak that softly.

I said I can't make it.

He brushes her hair out of her face, moves closer to her ear: It isn't hard, he nudges her gently, and the girl starts moving and he says: See?

Before heading into the woods she turns around, looks at the parked van as if that were the painful part, heading off and losing it, when just a couple of minutes earlier she wanted to get out and run.

Careful where you put your feet. It's not far, don't worry.

What isn't far?

It's a surprise.

My mother wasn't in the mood to talk, so I did instead: I told her a joke – she tried laughing – then I told her I was sorry that the holidays were almost over, I said again that I would've liked a scooter, that it would've been much easier for everyone.

'Now's not the time,' she said. 'And you'll be able to drive soon, anyway.'

'Not for two years still.'

'Two years are nothing, Elia. You're growing so fast. It feels like only yesterday you were this big' – she straightened her arm, holding her hand up to the edge of the table.

She suddenly asked me about Stefano, without mentioning Anna. 'Do you still see him?'

'Sometimes.'

She sighed, then turned to look outside.

A steep section, branches whipping her arms and face: the girl flails her hands, as if trapped in a spider's web.

I can't see anything.

My father raises the torch. Everything's fine, he says, I'm right here.

The path keeps getting harder. No one can help her, no one knows where she is.

What? he asks, when she stops.

I can't go on.

She hears him snort: Move it.

I can't, it's too narrow.

He passes her and moves the branches away, breaks one and shows her, she bends her back, hides her head in her arms and clamps her eyes shut.

I don't want to hurt you, he says, after a moment of silence. He seems shocked, stunned. We need to move. It's not safe here.

She could scream, she thinks, but who would hear her? She could tell him she won't take another step, but she doesn't want to anger him. *It's not worth it, it's a nightmare, you'll wake up soon.*

Please, he squeaks in falsetto, milady can proceed now.

There's something cold in his voice, something looming.

My mother made some coffee as I finished eating. Pale, hair undone, the palm trees on her dress about ready to fall off.

She went to the door. I thought she was about to leave but she stopped: 'There's something different in the air tonight.'

'What?'

'It feels like rain.'

The clear sky, stars. Warm breeze.

'I don't think so.'

'I wouldn't mind it,' she said. 'It'd be a nice change.'

She poured herself some coffee and looked at me, slightly lost, cup in hand, so I went into the lounge and switched on the TV.

A couple of minutes later she phoned Ida.

She trips up the winding path – stones and roots, fallen branches and piles of leaves – arms in front of her.

I can't, I need to stop.

No, he replies.

He breathes on her neck and starts pushing her again.

Please, she says.

I said no.

*   *   *

Ida arrived a little later with Simona. She brought a tub of ice cream. My mother put it in some glasses and we ate it under the porch, sitting on the swing chair, Simona on one of the steps.

They spoke of that torrid summer, the flowers dying in their pots. They said nothing about my father.

Simona stirred the ice cream, let it melt and drank it and it dribbled onto her T-shirt. My mother ran to fetch a sponge to help her clean it up, but she shook her head, grumbling, and Ida said: 'Leave it, Marta.' Then she slapped a hand on my knee. 'So, what's new with you?'

'Nothing new.'

'I saw you this morning,' she said.

'Where?'

'The petrol station.'

My mother, crouched over Simona, turned to look at me, tip of her tongue between her lips.

The darkness is suffocating.

He undoes his shirt. They're going down now, after an incline that made them slow down and climb.

I want to go home, she says.

She keeps repeating the same things, over and over.

Can you shut up?

The girl falls silent, finally, only her breathing, the scraping of their feet. He listens closely and, hiding under the whistling of the wind, he can hear the stream further down. The smell of water and mud.

We're almost there.

At that moment she trips on a stone or a root, falls forward, bursts into tears.

Can you be careful?

He holds her by the waist and hoists her up, a dead weight.

You're not hurt, are you?

The girl's mouth is open, her hands filthy, her jeans torn at the knee, marks of a grazing. She touches her right arm, moaning, and he remembers the dog tied to the tree, how it whined, desperate.

I asked you if you're hurt – but her reply is just another whine so he smacks his lips, points the light in her face, and the girl puffs out her cheeks, her chest shakes with the gagging, she vomits.

Oh Christ, he says, taking a step back. What's up with you? That's disgusting.

She's vomited over herself, on her T-shirt and shoes and her hair. She lifts her head slowly, wiping her mouth – she's still sobbing – and she throws herself against him, punches and slaps, so he grabs her wrists and shakes her.

What the fuck are you doing?

He manages to stop her, holds her tight in his arms, tells her: Calm down, it's no use.

The girl's face dives into his chest.

Calm down. Calm.

It takes her forever to quieten down. She stinks of vomit and she's wet and covered in mud.

Don't try that again. I'm here to help you.

She says something – lips and teeth scratching against his chest, as if trying to bite him – and he loosens his hold a little, asks her to repeat herself. The torch has fallen to the ground and is lighting up a bush. Water seems to be running under his feet now.

Let me go, you fucker, she says, and he sighs, exasperated.

You do what I say from now on. And don't call me that again. In any case, I forgive you.

He holds her tighter again, so she can understand. There is nowhere but the place they're headed for and his mind is running faster. There is nothing worth going back to.

We watched Ida and Simona walk up the drive: they crossed over and disappeared, then came the music.

I picked up a drop of ice cream from the bottom of my glass with a finger and licked it.

My mother was sitting next to me: she was staring at the spot where my father had started leaving the van.

I thought about Anna, in the corner of the kitchen, the light on the wall behind her.

I felt her lips on the palm of my hand.

People

'So, what happened yesterday?' asked my mother, before leaving for work.

I was still half asleep, eyelids heavy, my feet caught in the bedsheet: 'I missed the bus, I told you.'

'Were you with that kid?'

'Yeah.'

'Why didn't you call me?'

'I didn't think about it. Sorry.'

She picked up a pair of jeans from the floor, shook them, draped them over the back of a chair and ironed them out with her hand. I was watching her back, those focused and delicate movements in a sliver of light.

'You know what I was thinking, when you came back?'

'No.'

She didn't turn round. 'How different things might be if we didn't live up here.'

'Where do you want to live?' I asked her, leaning up on my elbows.

We never spoke about moving anywhere.

'Somewhere without all this silence,' she said.

I pulled the sheet over my nose, as soon as she left, and what had happened between me and Anna, in her father's car, emerged like the vivid and deceptive fragment of a dream. It took me a second to realise that was all it was. I thought I could smell her perfume on my T-shirt, in my hair.

I curled up on my other side and drifted off, floating on the surface. Then the phone rang.

She'd found the number on the bedside table, she said, as she was tidying up – the note I gave Stefano.

'I would've hung up if someone else had answered.'

'No one's home,' I said.

I sat on the floor, my back to the wall. I'd never heard her voice on the phone before and it sounded low and fragile.

'What were you doing?' she asked.

'Nothing. Where's Stefano?'

'Out. I think he went to buy cigarettes. I'd just like him to ask me for money. I'd give it to him, even if I don't have much left.' She sighed. 'I haven't slept, you know.'

'I have.'

'Lucky.' She cleared her throat, moving the mouthpiece away. 'I wanted to ask you a favour.'

I stretched out my legs on the floor and looked at my

long, skinny feet. Whatever she asked, I would have done it in a heartbeat. I would've run down to Ponte at that very moment, if that's what she wanted; I would've taken her to the beach or the falls, where no one ever went. But what would Stefano have said, what would I have told him?

'What happened yesterday . . .' she continued.

'Yes.'

'I want you to forget it.'

I folded my knees to my chest and squeezed them with my arm.

'Elia? You still there?'

'Didn't you like it?'

She let out a tired laugh and said: 'You can't ask me that.'

'Is that it, though?'

'No.'

'So what, then?'

'It's wrong,' she said. She slotted in another coin. 'You have to promise me you won't think about it again. Can you promise me that?'

I could hear my heart buzzing in my ears. I rested my head on the small table and murmured: 'Why?'

'What did you say, sorry?'

'Nothing. I said OK.'

'Everything like before, then?'

'I don't know.'

'Of course. I need to go now.'

'Can I come over later?'

'You can do what you want,' she replied, then hung up.

I stayed sitting on the floor for quite some time, receiver in hand, thinking about the words she'd just said, that laughter, the promise I made her, feeling like an idiot.

The birds singing, out there.

I got up and went into the yard. I started running, all of a sudden; I reached the edge of the woods and I stopped.

My head was spinning and I lay down, the ground and warm grass under the tips of my fingers.

I went back to the car, to the previous night – she'd said: 'Wait'. And I'd closed the door.

I thought my life had taken another direction, at that moment, and that I was no longer the same and I'd never go back again and that's how it went, in the end: life changes, and whatever you knew disappears behind you.

But not just *my* life . . .

Our life, the one that no one, other than ourselves, still cared about.

I didn't find her that afternoon.

Stefano was asleep on the sunbed. There were no sounds coming from the house. The shutters were closed.

I stood there, watching him, thinking about how to handle this, and he woke up, stretched his arms and yawned.

'I didn't hear you,' he said.

'I just got here. You alone?'

He nodded.

'Your mother?'

'I dunno. What do you care?'

I wanted to tell him it was my business too, now, that I was in it too. 'Want to go somewhere?' I said instead.

'Sure. In a second.'

I sat next to him on the grass, sun in our faces.

'I think I dreamed about you,' he said, and started picking at a mosquito bite, making it bleed, then wiped his hands on his jeans.

'What was I doing?'

'You were coming over here in your father's van.'

'That it?'

'I can't remember. Wait.'

I watched the white wall and it looked like it was burning.

'Oh yeah, you were driving.'

Two days later I saw her again as she was coming home carrying a shopping bag and I had just left her house.

'It's good to see you,' she said. Almost embarrassed.

'Same.'

'Everything going OK?'

'More or less.'

'I'm sure it is.' She squeezed the bag in her arms. 'OK,

bye then. I need to go and put this away.' I watched her walk inside, without looking back.

Before I reached the paved area, I heard her call me and I turned around. She was in front of me, biting her thumb.

'I'm not an idiot. I get it,' I said.

She curved her lips into her sad smile, raised a hand and looked at its palm. 'The life line is short,' she said.

'So?'

She showed me. 'See? It's this one. It says how much time we have left. A neighbour taught me. It came back to me today. She told me our life is entirely in our hands. Give me yours. Not that one, the left one.'

She took it and looked at it closely, pressing her wet thumb against my palm.

'Look how far it goes.' But I was looking at her, her eyes narrowed in the wind.

She lifted her head and noticed. 'You need to believe in it,' she said.

'I've never heard of this.'

She went back to studying my hand. 'What I told you, on the phone. Sometimes you know what you have to do but you don't do it. Maybe you can't. Maybe it's not that bad. We're just people, right?'

I said yes, but I wasn't sure what she meant.

'The best things are the hardest,' she added. 'Even if I've only had a few.' Then she looked behind her, looked down at the paving, brought her index finger to her mouth, kissed it and ran it over my lips.

I thought about her on the bus and as I was walking home, as I was walking across the porch, along the hallway, and lying down on my bed.

The sun was setting.

Had she changed her mind? All I wanted was to see her again and ask her.

My father stepped out of the bathroom, naked and dripping, stopping in front of my room, sun-baked arms drooping by his sides, his stomach white and bloated, his penis flaccid, saying: 'Someone took my clothes.' He moved his gaze to the photo of the boy and repeated: 'Someone.'

He didn't touch dinner. He just smoked, in shorts and a vest, one shoe on, the other foot naked.

'Have you lost it?' asked my mother.

'I'm from a different planet.'

'And don't they eat, where you're from?'

He shook his head.

Only then did I notice the scratches on his arms, because she looked at them, confused. She didn't ask anything. She started talking about what had happened that after-noon, her meeting with the boy's mother, in the square.

'I don't think she recognised me.' She was in bad shape, my mother said, skin and bone, her hair so thin and grey and her eyes empty. She was only thirty-one. 'If only they'd caught that monster. But they'll catch him eventually, somehow.'

Her faith, her blind optimism: tighter and more complicated knots than I could imagine at the time.

I cleaned my plate, got up, and my father moved his chair back and raised an arm to stop me. 'I didn't give you permission.'

My mother looked at us, trying to smile. 'Ettore, he's finished,' she said.

'If he doesn't ask me, he's not moving from here.'

We all stayed in silence, still, the air around us starting to crackle. I was watching the tense muscles in my father's face, his profile, his neck and jaw, as he stared at the wall.

'May I?' I said, in the end.

Once I had left them alone, he said: 'Don't contradict me.' His voice slid along the hallway and under my door. He wasn't shouting, he didn't seem angry. He even started laughing.

'I know what's going on in that little head of yours,' he added.

'Darling, please.'

'I see things you can't even imagine.'

'So try telling me about them.'

'It wouldn't help.'

I switched on the tape player, brought it onto the bed and turned up the volume.

*   *   *

He left in the van.

My mother came into my room, gestured to me to turn it down. 'I'm going to Ida's, I need to talk to her.' She was staring at the floor, a point somewhere in the middle of the room.

'You shouldn't let him get to you,' she said, raising her head. Then, 'Your hair's too long. You should get a haircut.'

'I like it like this.'

It was the same length as Stefano's.

'When you were smaller I used to cut it for you, remember?'

'I'm older now.'

'That's the way things go,' she said.

I stayed lying down for a little longer, then I went into their bedroom.

On my father's bedside table I found a half-empty packet of cigarettes: I took one and went out to smoke on the porch, the stars shining, the dirty cloth of a cloud. I was thinking about Anna, about what I'd ask her the next day – even though that was not how it went.

I threw out the butt, went back to my room and switched the tape player back on.

A couple of minutes later I heard a muffled sound.

'Mum?'

I popped my head into the hallway. There was only

moonlight. It wasn't her, I thought, it wasn't anything, but I heard it again: it was coming from the garage.

'Dad?'

I hadn't noticed him coming home.

I opened the door onto the stairs, went down a few steps and crouched down. The light was off but the main door must have been open: I caught a glimpse of my father's legs, his head and hands. He was sitting on the sofa, bent over, a bag between his feet: he was stuffing something in it.

'Who's there?' He stopped.

'It's me,' I replied.

'What do you want?'

'I heard a noise.'

He straightened up, and with the tip of his shoe shoved the bag away, across the dirty floor.

'Go to sleep,' he said.

X.

That was the place, the falls – but they got there via a riskier path that I didn't know.

We're here.

She complains, says her arm hurts and raises it, holding her elbow with her hand.

You can move it. You're OK.

I think it's broken.

I said you can move it.

He guides her to the stream, a short, steep track, downhill, wet ground and damp grass. He aims the light at the rocks, the fallen tree, the trees on the other bank.

Ever been here? he asks, but she keeps complaining.

Ever been here, I said?

The girl shakes her head, the corners of her mouth turned downwards, her face dirty with tears and dust.

Sit here, he says, and points at the tree. Rest a bit. Wait.

*   *   *

My father disappears behind her.

The girl hears him talking to himself, over the running stream, moving something – rocks? She doesn't turn round: too much fear. She clenches her teeth and shuts her eyes as the pain coils around her forearm and runs towards her shoulder and neck. She prays she'll be somewhere else when she opens her eyes again: at home or on the road down to Ponte, or with Simona, on the lounge floor colouring in a picture.

The stench of her own vomit clings to her nostrils.

She hears my father's footsteps again and, as he sits next to her, the light of the torch flashes against her closed eyelids.

Miss? Are you comfortable enough?

On those evenings when he came home late, or went out again after dinner, he would go to the plant or to the falls.

He was sure he was being followed, sure they were looking for him, and he felt safer by the water, down by the rocks.

He'd brought what he thought he'd need: batteries, a waterproof sheet, a knife, tape, cans of beer and food, a fork, a change of clothes. Everything stuffed into two bags hidden under a pile of stones, behind a bush by that tree trunk.

He just waited.

Come get me if you can.

The cry of a bird. Something rustling in the trees. He'd look around, but they would never find him, he knew that, so he'd calm down and drink.

On the edge of the pool – he told my mother – he'd sometimes start screaming into the silence, to prove he wasn't afraid, and his cries suddenly moved the stars and the wind, the leaves and the water and the creatures, the white, tired face of the moon. In those moments, he was God.

One of those evenings he took the knife and jabbed its tip into the palm of his hand. He cut without feeling any pain, sucking up the blood as his thoughts rushed fast, shining in the darkness, disappearing and reappearing – his dog's grave, the chimneys of the plant and the conspiracy, the letters he'd written. My mother. Me.

And the girl dancing and inviting him into the house: she understood him and wanted to tell him not to feel alone, and now she was sitting, crooked mouth and eyes closed, an arm against her chest, and he asked her: 'Miss? Are you comfortable enough?'

She doesn't reply: her breathing is interrupted by sobs.

If you're thirsty there's something to drink, he says. He gets out two cans and hands her one, but she shakes her head.

All right, I'll put it down here, on the ground. We're safe, stop crying.

He rests the torch on the trunk. I never brought anyone else here, if that's what you're thinking. Never, I swear.

He opens his can and takes a drink. His hands are shaking again: the beer runs down his chin. He wipes his mouth and looks at the sky.

The stars are moving from one point to the other, the moon swings in the dark. It's a sight, and it's all thanks to him: he starts laughing and the girl jumps, moves aside as if he were about to hit her, so he laughs harder.

So dramatic, he says. Come back here.

He throws his head back and drinks again. Once he's finished, he crumples the can in his fist and chucks it into the distance.

The girl touches her arm, rotates her wrist slightly.

See? he says. Nothing wrong.

He lights himself a cigarette, takes the torch, aims it at the pool and turns to look at the water.

He smokes in silence.

I know, he says after a while. It's true.

He seems sad, as he keeps repeating: I know. Then he switches off the torch and everything is plunged into darkness.

The girl whines, bends forwards.

Better this way, he says. You never know.

He picks up the other can, opens it, hands it to her. Drink.

I can't, she sobs.

Yes, you can. I'll help you. Lift your head.

He brings it to her lips and tilts it upwards. Come on, he says, and she takes a gulp and starts coughing.

Slowly, not like that.

She takes another gulp.

I have everything we need, trust me. If he comes here, everything is set.

He tells her about his knife and she starts screaming, spitting out an acid spurt that rises from her chest.

He presses a hand down on her mouth, the other on the back of her head, and holds her like that, until she calms down.

Do you want him to hear you? Do you want him to find us?

The girl is only able to say: Enough.

Don't scream then, he says.

He takes out of his pocket what he picked up from the van, rests it on the fallen tree.

I don't understand you, you know that?

He stretches out his legs and undoes his trousers.

The Right Moment

The first week of August, the sky was constantly pale and the wind scorched the skin. A fire broke out at the old mine: they found two tanks of petrol in one of the shacks. The flames burned down the wooded area and the red and white tape next to the slope.

The river flowed slow and murky. In front of the beach, like a mirage, an island appeared.

The library closed for the summer holidays. My mother became slow and tired. She'd walk into a room with a cloth in her hand and look around, as if searching for something to clean, then she'd turn and leave. She'd sit at the table, dirty dishes in the sink, touching her hair, wiping her fingers on her brow.

'Mum, what's up?'

'It's the heat. I can't take it any more,' she'd say.

'Same here.'

She'd stare at me and sigh. 'Everything's out of place. Everything's messed up.'

'It doesn't matter.'

'Yes, it does.'

She stopped reading – 'I can't focus'. She'd collapse onto the sofa, after dinner, in front of the TV, slowly opening her eyes and dragging herself into the kitchen when my father came back from his outings, then go to her bedroom and immediately fall asleep.

One early morning I heard Ida telling her: 'It'll be over soon, Marta, you'll see.'

My mother replied: 'I don't know what to do.'

That apathy lasted for days – her clouded gaze and the sleep to which she had to surrender. But maybe it kept her afloat: the empty, silent space where she fell at night, as my father drifted off and she wasn't able to reach him.

I was sleeping badly, on the other hand. I'd wake up hearing my father's voice, his footsteps in the hallway.

I'd think of Anna in those moments – she had been avoiding me since the day she asked me to show her the palm of my hand. *You need to believe in it*, she'd said.

In the dark, I imagined taking her up to the stream, then I'd hear my father's footsteps and I turned to face the wall, holding my hands over my ears.

*   *   *

One afternoon Stefano and I went back to the falls. We didn't jump in – there was only a trickle of water coming down off the rocks. We cooled down in the pool for a while. I gave him a brief lesson: 'Move your arms like this, your legs like this.'

'You know what?' he said. 'I almost like you.'

'Course you do. Where else would you find someone like me?'

'I said *almost*.'

As we dried off, he saw three open cans behind the tree trunk.

'Hey, look at this.' He went closer, took one and shook it. 'Someone else comes up here,' he said.

'Looks like it.'

'Damn. I like being here alone with you.' He puckered his lips and blew me a kiss.

I hit him with my T-shirt.

We burst out laughing.

'Dickhead,' I said.

I only briefly thought of my father: it could've been anyone at all.

One evening he came home, trousers drenched. He was still working at the time. He showed up in the lounge, looking at his hands. My mother just said: 'Go and get changed.'

He disappeared behind the door.

I asked her: 'Where's he been?'

'I have no idea.'

'Did you see his trousers?'

She rested her head against the armrest, curled up and pointed at the screen. 'What's this film about? I still don't get it.'

'You were sleeping.'

'Really?'

'Yeah.'

'I might go to bed then.'

She put on her slippers and went to brush her teeth.

That night my father opened my bedroom door, came closer and leaned over, touching my shoulder.

'Up,' he whispered.

I stayed perfectly still, eyes shut.

'I said up.'

'What is it, Dad?'

He murmured: 'You need to come now.' He threw the sheet off me, grabbed my wrist, dragged me into the kitchen and out of the house. I tried complaining but he just dragged harder.

'Shut up and walk.'

We crossed the grass, headed for the woods. Just a pale light in the sky. My father was breathing with his mouth open. He was talking to himself. Suddenly he stopped, clicked his tongue two or three times, like a signal, then stuttered: 'Now look around. Who did all this?'

I imagined the house behind me, shrouded in darkness, my mother still asleep. The empty road. Ida's house.

'Who did what?' I tried freeing myself, but he just tugged harder.

'Answer me. Who did it?'

'You're hurting me.' I was trying not to cry. *Don't you dare, you're not a baby.*

'Answer the question.'

'Dad, I don't understand.'

He came closer, his breath sour and hot, and looked me straight in the eye: 'Your father knows the truth.' Then he grazed my brow with a kiss. 'Come on. We have a way to go yet.'

At that moment I heard a door slam and I turned around. The lights were on and I saw my mother's silhouette next to the car, in her white pyjamas.

'Ettore?' she called.

He let me go and she ran towards us.

'Oh God,' she said, panting, as she reached us. 'What are you doing out here?'

She ran her eyes over the wall of trees: my father was looking in that direction and she thought – or maybe wanted to think – that he had seen or heard something, that he had come out to check, taking me with him. 'What happened?'

That's when I started crying. I lowered my head,

shoulders shaking with the sobbing, and I clenched my fists. I wanted to tell her: *It was him* – but *him* was my father.

She looked at me and asked him: 'Can you tell me why you're out here?'

Her voice had steadied a bit.

'I wanted to teach him a couple of things.'

'At this hour?'

'It was the right moment.'

My mother didn't reply. Wisps of her hair were blowing in the wind.

She took my hand. 'We're going back to bed.'

Only later did she tell me she'd woken up gasping, scared, thinking 'I'm alone,' and 'Where's Elia?' She had come into my room and found the empty bed.

'We still have some time before morning,' she said, stroking my hair. 'Try sleeping now.'

I'd stopped crying, but I was shaking.

'Mum?'

'Yes?'

I opened my lips but nothing came out, as if he'd dragged me to the middle of the woods, left me alone, and I'd got lost.

'You need to try and understand him,' she said. 'You need to try. There are some people who feel things differently from others. Your father is one of them.' She tucked the sheet over my shoulders. 'Losing his job was a bad thing.'

'But he found another,' I said.

'Maybe it's not enough. Maybe it's not even that.'

'He scared me.'

'He'd never hurt you, Elia. He'd never do that, not for anything in the world.'

She kissed me goodnight, then stopped in the doorway. I thought she wanted to add something, but she closed the door and left. It was only then that I realised she hadn't asked me anything, not a single question about what happened. *What did he tell you? Where did he want to go?*

I immediately heard their voices from the yard.

My father burst out laughing.

She said: 'I really don't think that's appropriate.'

Then she started laughing too, anyway, as if it were her last chance – both together, both awake – and I thought nothing else in the world mattered to my mother, and at the time I didn't realise what she'd done, it didn't seem enough.

I remember a restless sleep – noises, birdsong, the phone ringing. It was quite late when I woke up. My mother was in the kitchen, in her pyjamas.

'Where is he?' I asked.

She frowned, like she didn't understand the question.

'Dad.'

'Oh. He went to work. How are you feeling?'

'My head hurts.'

'Eat something. You'll feel better.'

Her eyes were baggy, dark, deep rims under them.

'Someone called earlier,' she said. 'But they didn't say anything.'

Anna, I thought.

My mother went to the window, leaned outside. Then she turned round and crossed her arms. 'Listen, why don't you go and stay with a friend tonight? Isn't that a good idea?'

She smiled. She kept her feelings to herself.

'OK,' I replied.

I already knew where I wanted to go.

This is what she'd been doing, that time: bringing me back to safety, watching over me until morning, until my father – the man she would never stop loving – left. Then she sent me away, as the invisible flames rose, as the house burned to ash.

They were left alone.

I don't know what happened, between them, that night. I don't know what was said.

She always refused to talk about it.

XI.

She watches as he undoes his trousers – something she doesn't want to believe – taking off his shoes, socks, standing up and undressing, leaving nothing on but his underwear.

She sees his shadow walk towards the water, crouch down and plunge his hands in, splash his chest and face.

What happened to you? he says. You don't trust me any more. What, did they get to you? Did they try telling you things?

Now the pain has moved down to her wrist. Her lips are dry, her legs cold and stiff. She closes her eyes and he disappears into the darkness.

Did you get in the van on purpose? Were you colluding with that guy?

She pushes her tongue against her teeth, moves it around her cheeks, says: You're the one who gave me a lift, fucker.

He shakes his head.

I told you I don't want to hear that word again. I'd be more careful if I were you.

He pours some water onto his hair, pulls it back.

That time, when you were dancing and you gestured for me to come and join you, were they also there in the house?

What are you talking about?

She tastes something sweet in her mouth, the taste of blood: she has just bitten her own lip.

He walks back, slowly, stops in front of her, his body half naked, massive, terrifying.

Why did you do it? he asks.

He stutters over his words. Punches his leg.

So now what? How am I supposed to feel? Tell me.

Let me go, she says. I swear I won't tell anyone.

No.

I swear.

Shut up, you know nothing. Nothing about me. I thought you did, but no, no one understands how I feel.

I do understand.

He bursts out laughing.

Fucking liar, he says. At this point, all I can do is wait.

Please.

It's pointless.

He bends over the fallen tree, grabs the thing he took out of his pocket.

Turn around, he tells her.

Metal wire: he'd picked some up from his garage, made a spool, chucking it in the back of the van.

They might find me.
I might need it.

The girl suddenly jumps up, runs past him and towards the path, shouting, stumbling blindly. He catches her immediately, the wire still in his hand, and drags her back, as she kicks and struggles.

Sit down.

He shoves her onto the tree, undoes the spool, pulls her arms behind her back, wraps the wire around her wrists. It's not easy; she's struggling to free herself.

I don't want to make it too tight, he says. Just a little.

She shouts: You're crazy. Oh God, please. What are you going to do to me?

He stops for a second.

That's what they told you. And you believe them, I suppose.

Piece of shit, she's able to scream, then her voice is suffocated by uncontrollable sobbing.

He goes back to where he's hidden his stuff, pulls the knife out from a bag, studies the shiny grey blade, puts it down on a rock, takes out the tape, rips off a strip and approaches her from behind, quietly, grabbing her by her hair and placing it over her mouth.

I loved you, he says, hearing the girl whine, then he heads to the pool and leaves her there, voiceless, terrified. The taste of her own blood. The stench of her own vomit. Her tears.

He hits himself, sharp and hard, growling like a dog – what was left of my father? Was that still him?

What the fuck do I do now?

Then he calms down, and his slaps get weaker and he loses his strength, his arms fall to his sides.

He looks up to the sky.

Tell me.

He takes off his underwear and dips his feet in the water.

The Good Life

My mother asked me who I was staying with and I gave her a random name. She nodded, but I think she knew. Maybe she didn't care, at least at that moment: wherever I was, it would've been fine.

I stuffed my pyjamas and toothbrush into a bag.

She followed me out to the porch.

'Have fun,' she said.

I imagined the house where I lived growing smaller and further away, out of reach, as I pulled out bits of seat stuffing, sitting at the back of the bus.

Anna was in the garden, her hair hidden by a blue scarf, with a pair of rubber gloves and a bucket. She was pouring out some dirty water onto the grass.

'Hi,' she said, then hesitated, and frowned. 'What happened?'

I moved closer and showed her the bag. 'Can I stay here tonight?'

She thought about it for a second. 'You can stay as long as you like.' She put the bucket down on the grass, removed her gloves and looked at the sky. 'No air today, right?'

We pulled out the bed, she put the pillowcase and sheets in the wash and gave me some clean ones. 'I'll sleep on the sofa,' she said.

There was a lounge next to the kitchen, its shutters always closed, dark furniture covered in dust and a small broken TV.

'I can sleep there.'

'I think not.'

We ate, then Stefano, who still hadn't asked me anything, said: 'Let's go for a walk.'

We got to the playground and sat on the bench next to the swings for a smoke. The air was clearer: we saw a couple of foamy clouds gather in the sky. Insects were buzzing. It was sunset.

'Did they kick you out?'

I pictured the boy, his legs stretched out, hands fastened to the chains – he was staring at me.

Stefano elbowed me, taking a drag. 'Hey, you listening to me?'

'I'm not deaf.'

'So?'

I took a deep breath and told him about my father,

about last night – how he'd dragged me outside, what he told me, 'Your father knows the truth.'

'Ever since he lost his job he's been doing weird things.'

I told him about his letters, his insomnia, the windows of the van, the shredded newspapers.

'One time he said he was God.'

'Holy shit.'

'Yeah.'

'Maybe it's true, though.' He chuckled and started biting a nail.

'It's not a joke.'

'OK.'

'It's not funny.'

'I know. But why didn't you tell me sooner?'

'If you keep things to yourself they don't seem as real.'

He nodded. 'It doesn't change anything, though,' he said. 'Even if you don't talk about it. Things still happen.'

I could hear the river running behind us, the smell of water carried to us on the wind.

'And before? What was he like before?' he asked, and at that moment my father emerged from the darkness: I saw him cross the playground, a giant figure, and disappear again.

'He was funny. He'd get pissed off about nothing some-times, or he just stopped talking for some reason and I didn't understand why, but he was funny.'

A car's headlights flashed in the dark.

'Why didn't you tell him to fuck off?'

'I dunno.'

'It's a bit of shitty situation, Tex,' he said, then he put out his cigarette, stood up, shoved his hands in his pockets and kicked the bench.

'What's up with you?'

'I called him yesterday,' he said.

My father and his, as if they were linked. As if *we* were linked, now. He hadn't talked to me about him in a while, and I hadn't asked.

'And what did he say?'

'That it's better if we stay here for a bit. As soon as he can, he'll send us some money. He says he's met someone who can give him work.'

'What kind of work?'

'Removals. Funny, right?'

He kicked the bench again.

'Is he coming to see you at least?'

'It's just a bunch of shit,' he said.

He walked to the slide and climbed it. When he reached the top, he struck his chest and raised his fists to the sky.

'I am God,' he shouted, and I started laughing.

I woke up at dawn.

I didn't recognise the room. Then I turned to one side and saw Stefano sleeping, an arm across his head.

I'm safe. I thought about Anna, lying on the sofa.

The wind was blowing against the walls: I listened to it for a while, then I got up, quietly opened the door, shut it behind me and went to the bathroom, where the shutters were open.

The first morning light was dripping down from the sky.

As I peed I looked at a piece of soap on the edge of the bathtub, then I flushed, drank from the tap and went back into the hallway.

That's when I heard her: she was humming. She was in the kitchen – the light was on, just a white rim around the door – and I stopped for a second, my heart in my throat, before I decided to join her.

She was sitting with her elbows on the table: she turned her head and looked at me, as if she'd been waiting.

'Already up?' she asked.

'Yep.'

'I couldn't sleep either.'

'Was it me? Did I make too much noise?'

She shook her head, smiling. She was wearing a flowery nightgown, long to her feet. The flowers were vivid in the light, as if I could grab them in my hands.

'I made coffee, want some?'

'Please.'

'How's the bed?'

'Comfy.'

'The sofa isn't bad either,' she said.

She poured coffee into a cup, got out the sugar, a teaspoon, set them on the table. 'You hungry?'

'No.'

She sat next to me. She smiled again, as I was drinking. 'I don't want to know what happened to you,' she said.

'OK.'

'But it'll pass, Elia. That's not just a saying. It's normal.'

'What is?'

'Being confused.'

She looked up at the ceiling, bit her lip. Her eyes looked like she was about to cry. 'Do you want to hear a story?'

'Yeah.'

'Well, when my mother died, my father called me. He wanted me to come to the funeral. I'd given him my number, two months earlier, I'd called to tell him I was sorry, that I was confused, that I felt . . . I don't know. Tired. They didn't even know I'd had a baby. Can you believe that?'

I shrugged.

'I don't know why I did it, why I followed him, I mean. I wonder what I was thinking. Do you know what he used to do?'

'No.'

'Door-to-door sales. Encyclopaedias. That's how I met him. He showed up here, then left and came back a couple of days later. He took me for a ride. He'd say: 'You're special, you deserve more.' Blah blah blah. He already lived by himself. That's where I went, his place. He had others after me. All special, I imagine. He lost that job, and many others. At a certain point I couldn't stand it any longer. And when my father called me, after she . . . I couldn't bear coming back. It was so absurd. I couldn't forgive myself. But here I am. What matters is he let us stay.'

She took my left hand and turned it, palm facing upwards.

'Remember what I told you? That you'll have a long life? And look, you'll be happy.'

'Where do you see that?'

'Trust me,' she said.

'And you?'

She grimaced and let my hand go, went towards the door, opened it and looked outside, the warm light of dawn.

'Does your mother know you came here?'

'No.'

'Right. It's going to be another hot one today.'

She closed the door again and leaned against it, so I asked her, a question buzzing round my head for quite some time.

'Did you like my dad?'

'Why do you want to know?'

'Just curious.'

'Your father was different. He was like me in a way. Sometimes he was so sad that I wanted to hug him, and other times he never stopped laughing and talking. We were friends. I'm sure your mother didn't like that.'

'I don't care what she thinks.' I stood up and went to stand with her by the door.

She said: 'Stop.' But she said it weakly, without looking me in the face.

I closed my hands around her waist, the smaller bones of her hips, and pulled her towards me. She squirmed away, pointing her feet, and I pulled her closer and hugged her, as if we were alone in a place no one else could reach.

'No,' she said.

'Why?'

'Because it's not possible.'

I held her for a while – the smell of sleep – I pushed her against the door and started grinding against her. She stood still, breathing with her mouth open, she moaned and closed her eyes, I leaned over and kissed her, driving my tongue against her teeth, and she grazed the tip of mine with hers, but then I felt her stiffen, she shook her head, said: 'Stop it.' She freed herself of me and went into the garden, the flowers on her nightgown floating in the dawn.

When I got back to the bedroom, legs weak, head spinning, as if I were one person and another and another again all together, Stefano kicked his sheet and grumbled something.

I know I shouldn't have, I thought, *but I couldn't help it.*

I lay down on the bed, clenching my teeth as the springs creaked, then I was still, my erection fading, the sound of his regular breathing, the shadows on the ceiling and the first birdsong, imagining her out there, as day broke.

XII.

He plunges into the pool, reaches the deepest point and then stops – this is how I picture him, this is how he still appears in my dreams.

He gathers some water in the palms of his hands, then he slips, gasping, but catches himself. He cups his hands again, fills them, stretches out his arms and looks ahead.

Footsteps. A man on the path.

I was hoping you'd come, says my father. Now I see you.

So do I, at last.

My father says: That's why I came. Then he shuts his eyes, pouring water over his brow, like a christening.

Were you waiting? says the man.

He nods.

Well, I was here before you. Did you think it was me, in the car? That I was following you?

My father shakes his head.

Who was it then?

Stupid fucking question.

The man brings a finger to his lips and looks behind him, then asks: Are you sure? Think about it. Who was it? And who am I?

They had met when he was a kid, when he was digging that hole in the woods behind his house – silent, standing next to him. Years later, while he was there at the stream with Anna Trabuio, my father dived in and curled up at the bottom of the pool, the light on the surface further and further away, and the man was there, both holding their breath together.

Anna had grabbed him by his armpits and dragged him out, exhausted. She asked him if he had meant to kill himself.

In front of the cotton plant, after he was fired, one late afternoon the man got into his van and they both waited for his colleagues to leave.

In the snow, they both watched the girl dancing, and he was behind him when he was writing those letters in the kitchen, on the worktop in the garage, in the back of the van.

One evening, next to him on the tree trunk, he'd handed him his knife and my father had cut his hand.

It was a secret, a presence he'd sometimes doubted, and one that abandoned him in the days when he fell to pieces, feeling like a failure, and could do nothing but sit on the porch for hours on end, or lie on the bed.

But now here he was, that was all that mattered.

The man steps forwards and is bathed in moonlight.

So? Are you not going to answer?

My father looks at him: for a second he's reminded of himself and that terrifies him. He rubs his eyes.

Who was it? Tell me.

You know, he replies.

But did you really see him?

The headlights of a car driving in the dark, following his van. The guy behind the windscreen.

Bullshit, he says.

Leave it alone. Think whatever you want.

My father asks: what do I have to do now?

The man picks up a branch, smacks it on his knee. Isn't that what you wanted? he says.

I thought you agreed.

I don't think I ever asked you. I never ask anyone anything. That's not how it works. You always do what you want.

My father's teeth chatter, he clutches his arms around his chest, rubs his hands on his shoulders.

Help me, he says.

Get out of there.

Fine. Then?

The man turns around and uses the branch to point at the girl, or at least that's what it looks like.

*   *   *

The pain in her wrists, the wire cutting the flesh. She can't breathe. Sweat and tears, and she can't wipe them. The tape is burning over her mouth.

Calm down, she tells herself. *Inhale.*

It should be happening much faster, whatever it is, but time is a black hole and she has fallen straight in.

The only thing she can think of is that light between the trees, the last house they passed, the dog barking.

She rubs her wrists against each other, uselessly.

She watches him gather some water and let it fall over his brow. She can hear him murmur, as if talking to someone. He rubs his shoulders, moves back to the shore and gets out.

The water was cold, he says. You did well to stay here.

He sits closer and the girl squirms, tries her wrists again.

Why are you fidgeting? he asks. Can't you just stay still?

Make him get dressed, she prays. *Make him let me go.*

He says: Look at me, running his fingers through her hair and down her cheek, a delicate gesture, almost a caress.

I said look. Please.

His livid feet. His open legs. His penis. His bloated stomach.

Do you see me? Am I not still me?

He takes the torch and shines it again.

Now turn around, he says, and aims the beam at the path.

Hey, he calls to him, but his voice echoes in the silence. He must've hidden himself, he thinks.

She hunches her back and clutches her knees to her chest.

Hey, can you hear me?

The man has gone. My father switches off the torch, lets it fall, hides his face in his hands. He imagines him walking along the path, then next to his van, then taking the road to Ponte. He imagines him far away, and then loses him. The car lights turn off, in his mind.

Listen, I need to tell you something, he says.

He sits thinking about it for a bit.

I don't know if there was someone following us. That's the truth. I think so, but maybe it was just in my mind.

He slaps a hand to his head, and she whispers: There was.

My father freezes.

What did you say?

There was someone.

He looks at her: You can speak? How?

You just need to want to.

He doesn't lose sight of her mouth, the strip of tape. He wonders if she might be teasing him, because this isn't possible, then a question comes to him.

Did you see who I was talking to?

I saw everything.

You only say that because you're afraid.

I was. Not any more, replies the girl.

Well, I'm glad.

He offers her a cigarette and she turns slightly, showing her wrists.

I forgot, sorry.

He lights one for himself.

Did you really want me to come in that night?

She nods, and he opens his arms, aims his hands at the trees and the stream and the sky: Who do you think did this? he asks, then points to himself.

It was you. Everything exists because of you.

My father takes off her shoes, picks up his shirt and trousers, he lays them out next to the tree. He thinks of the knife. The long waits in front of the plant. All the letters he wrote.

I feel tired, he says.

Me too.

Now they're both standing, both shaking. He points at the makeshift bed.

I'm sorry, it's not the comfiest. And I can't untie you.

I'm fine, she says.

Sunday

In the days that followed Anna became elusive again. She just asked: 'How are you?' when we passed each other, without looking me in the eye. She always had some chore to be taking care of.

Stefano and I went down to the beach, one afternoon – we sat by the river, in front of the new island, with another group of kids who had a radio. We shared food and cigarettes. We went for a swim, Stefano spotted a girl he fancied, started splashing her and she laughed. They got out of the water and walked away, and he whispered something in her ear.

Later, as we were drying in the sun, he asked me: 'How's things at home?'

I didn't know what to say.

He punched my shoulder. 'Bunch of shit, told you.'

He rarely spoke to his father, now, and fought less with his mother – sometimes he just ignored her, that's all – but before *Ferragosto*, just as the petrol station was closing, what he wasn't expecting was for his grandfather to ask him for help.

'Help with what?' I asked.

'Sorting out some stuff.'

'What stuff?'

The bedroom, for example.

'So I can sleep in it by myself,' he said. 'My mother can stay in the lounge, it could become her room. And he wants to paint everything and connect the phone again. He's not that much of an idiot after all.'

'So you're staying?'

'Just for a bit.'

'What about school?'

He pulled his hair down over his eyes and looked at its tips. 'I'm not going back, Tex. I'm not like you.'

I thought about the money, the brooch, and everything else, the coins in his pockets, Santo's probing eyes on him, but maybe he'd stopped stealing, because there was nothing else after that, or he never showed it to me.

It took them a whole week: they removed the wallpaper and Santo taught him how to use the roller. Stefano listened to him: all of a sudden the man seemed available, and Stefano found it strange working side by side, but he didn't mind it.

I spent more time at home, while they were busy redecorating. I stayed in my room, pretending to study or do my homework as I thought about Anna – I missed her. I listened to music, read my comics. I'd doze off, in the biting heat, a dreamless sleep, and would wake up imagining her next to me.

My mother was calm, or so she seemed, and always engrossed in something: she emptied the wardrobes and dusted the shelves, she cleaned the kitchen top to bottom, washed the curtains and grouted the tiles over the tub in the bathroom. Before dinner she'd go and visit Ida. In the evening she watched TV.

Once, though, I saw her walk down the drive, stop halfway and stare at our house as if she didn't recognise it.

I was on the porch, putting my shoes on.

She started walking again and, as she reached me, her eyes were teary and distant.

One Sunday, as the wind was lashing the branches, my father didn't leave the house. He took something out to the van, stayed a while wandering in the yard, his head low as if thinking about something, then he came back in and we sat down for food.

He looked at my mother and smiled.

'What?' she asked.

'Nothing.'

'What are you thinking?'

He turned around, looked at the grass behind the

window, put his fork down on his plate, and said: 'The grass is too long. I need to cut it today.'

The wind died down in the afternoon, the white sky and the air filled with the monotone whine of the lawnmower.

My father bare-chested, a pair of shorts, dark socks, work shoes, unshaven. My mother brought him a bottle of water. He stopped. They said something and kissed.

He finished within a couple of hours.

I was sitting at my desk when my father opened the door.

'Help me,' he said.

I followed him without a word, even though I didn't want to, and I saw two rakes against the wall.

'Take one,' he said.

We started raking the grass. I could hear his sighs, the intermittent groans of a tired man. I was thinking about that night when he dragged me out of the house, his questions, my mother coming to get me and how it all drove me to the Trabuios' kitchen, with Anna, at dawn.

Things in life always get mixed up – it wasn't a fully formed thought, then, just two memories overlapping in a hazy image. I wanted to run into town, but I wiped my forehead and kept raking.

When we finished, my father slipped a cigarette out from its packet, lit it and rested the handle of the rake against his side.

'At least you won't have to do this again for a while,' he said.

'Neither will you.'

'Yeah. Me neither.'

I know what he meant now: I didn't understand him that day.

He stared at me, tight-lipped, frowning.

'Can I go now?' I asked, uncomfortable.

He turned to look at the woods and I left.

That was the last thing I did with my father.

XIII.

It's been a long journey, but you're finally here.

You stop the van on the road, get out, lean on the bonnet. It's still dark. The lights are on at home: you watch them. You just want to rest.

You run your fingers through your hair, do up your shirt. Your hands are dirty, your shoes wet.

What have I done? you ask.

What will they think, what will you say?

You raise your eyes and see your wife, in the kitchen, at the window: she puts her hands to the glass, presses her face against it, like she's heard a noise. Then you see your son, next to her, and you go to wave, but they can't see you, can't know you're there.

You breathe. You watch the fixed stars, the sliver of moon.

You walk up the drive, up the steps to the door – they left it open, they were expecting you. You stop, you want to take off your shoes: at that moment you hear footsteps and see yourself appearing from the hallway, smiling calmly.

Darling, she says. Where did you get to?

I was in the garage. I didn't realise it was this late.

You sit down to eat. Just another evening. Just another family.

You open your mouth and try to say something, but your voice is trapped in your throat. What you want to say is: *I'm here.* That you've been out for too long – you can't even remember how long – but you're finally back. That you've missed them and you've never stopped loving them.

Try to understand.

You lean against the frame, exhausted, watching yourself eat and laugh and talk as though nothing has happened.

Forgive me.

Then you turn: the road and your front yard have gone. Just the water rushing under the rocks, the shadows of the trees, the pool, and the girl sitting on the tree trunk – she's crying – and so you leave, leave your home behind.

The things you loved disappear into darkness.

You have arrived where you are. This is what happened to you. There is no other explanation.

You reach out an arm, touching her cheek.

I'm really tired, you say, let's sleep, but the girl turns to one side, rest on an elbow, she sits up.

What are you doing? Come back down.

She moves clumsily, kneels – she looks like she's praying.

You should pick up the knife and show her. You should say, *Don't make me use it.*

I'll do it now, you think, but instead you just say, again: Come down.

The End of Summer

That night my mother called Ida, whispering on the phone. I was dozing on the sofa, so I can only imagine her: 'Sorry about the time, I woke you. I don't know where Ettore is, I don't know what to do.'

But Ida was still awake too. She told her of the girl. She'd received a call from the girl's parents: they were worried, she said, because their phone at home just kept ringing. They were hoping she was still there – some emergency with Simona – and that she'd forgotten to warn them.

'I got home late,' she added. 'She left in a hurry. If she'd missed the bus she would've asked me for a lift.'

'Right.'

'Maybe she walked home.'

'Maybe.'

'But she should've been home by now.'

My mother was struck by this, she told me much later, but it was a coincidence she didn't pay too much attention to, at the time. She focused on the girl, forcing herself to think he'd be back soon.

'Maybe she has a new boyfriend and they don't know,' my mother said. 'Maybe they're together and they haven't noticed what time it is.'

Neither spoke of Giorgio Longhi, of the monster still at large.

'And you?' asked Ida.

'I called the hospital.'

'He'll be back soon, you'll see.'

She knew about my father's odd hours and his after-dinner outings.

'But it's the middle of the night now.'

Ida changed the subject, to get her mind off things. 'Elia?' she asked.

'He's fallen asleep.'

'Good.'

I don't know if she connected the two things – my father and the girl – while they were on the phone, or whether it was later, still awake, that she started thinking about it. When my mother had told her about the letters, Ida told her he needed help. She replied that Ida was exaggerating: they'd argued for a couple of days and didn't talk or see each other for a bit.

'Do you think I should go and look for him?'

I imagine a pause.

'No, no. As soon as he arrives, just try talking to him.'

My mother listened.

She hung up the receiver and headed out, under that black, clear sky.

When my father arrived home, barefoot, with damp hair, an open shirt, he left the van in the yard. My mother took him to the kitchen – he was unsteady on his feet, swaying and tripping over.

I placed myself next to the fridge, back to the wall, and watched them.

'Sit down,' she told him. 'Where were you? What happened?'

She asked him why he'd taken off his socks and shoes. 'Are they still in the van?'

My father didn't reply.

'Darling, look at your arms. Your neck. And here, on your forehead. Did you have an accident?'

He started staring at the wall.

'We were worried sick,' she said, then looked up at me and nodded towards the door. 'Let me talk to your father.'

I went to his van. I looked at the windscreen, the bumpers, the lights, the sides, trying to find a dent, but found nothing.

The keys were still in the ignition. I opened the door and leaned in – the light inside was on – peering at the compartment in the back: his shoes weren't there.

I wandered round the yard, looking at the grass surfacing to the light. I could hear birds singing. I felt like my father was there, on the grass, and was waiting for me to join him.

Had he driven all night? Had he stopped somewhere?

I thought: *You're wrong if you think I care. That's enough now.*

I'd left the van door open and, before I closed it, I took one last look inside: there was a bag on the floor, under the passenger seat, as if someone had stuffed it under there.

I recognised it immediately.

Late that morning they came to get my father.

My mother followed them in her car.

Ida came to see me. She hadn't gone to work so she could stay home with Simona. She looked like she hadn't slept either.

I asked her about the girl.

No sign of her, she replied.

'Do you need anything?' she asked, as her daughter mumbled behind her. She said nothing about what had happened: my father and the *carabinieri* car. I don't think she knew, not yet, but by now she could imagine it.

She even tried joking. 'I told myself, let's go and bother him.'

I said I was fine, I didn't need anything, and she rubbed my shoulder: 'As you wish,' and she left.

*   *   *

When the phone rang I was in the bathroom. I ran to the hallway, picked up and said: 'Mum?'

There was silence, just the whistling of the wind, before Anna replied: 'It's me.'

I pressed the phone against my ear, my cheeks flushing, my heart skipping a beat. She said she'd heard *something*, when she was out shopping, something about us.

'Are you OK?' she asked, and sounded worried.

There was still nothing, to me, that felt irreparable, nothing that I had realised yet. I told her it was good to hear her – her voice in the distance, as if she were someplace I couldn't get to.

'Are you alone?'

'Yes.'

'Where are your parents?'

I told her what I knew – the *carabinieri* station – and she kept quiet, then asked: 'When did they head over?'

She didn't ask why – a question I would've asked, in her place.

'Before lunch.'

The empty house, my parents' bedroom door wide open, the unmade bed, the bundled sheets.

'My father never came back last night. He only showed up this morning.'

'What happened?'

I told her I had no idea.

I didn't tell her about the bag, not then – I kept it to

myself even with Ida and my mother. I didn't say that, as the sun rose, I'd picked it up, peeked inside, found the carton of cigarettes, took out a packet, hid it behind a flowerpot and put the bag back there, under the seat.

My father must've given her a lift. But how was it possible that the girl hadn't noticed, that she hadn't called, saying: 'I think I left my bag in your van. I don't know where my head is.'

My mother had joined me, she'd leaned over the bumper.

'It looks fine, right?'

The singing of birds sounded like a really distant sobbing.

'Try getting some sleep now. Your father and I are going to bed.'

'Then they came to get him,' I told her.

A car, the doors slamming, someone knocking.

My parents were still in bed, I was in my room. My mother went to open the door. I heard a man say: 'Good morning, we're looking for your husband.' My father joined them: 'Here.' A chair dragged across the floor. A lighter flicked.

I kept listening – low voices – then I headed for the kitchen.

There were two *carabinieri*. The younger man looked like a kid in a fake uniform: he waved at me and smiled, almost embarrassed, took off his hat and wiped his sweat.

The other, tall and well built, legs wide, kept his eyes on my father. I'd seen them often in Ponte, but in our house they looked different, like strangers.

My father was sitting, still barefoot, his scratched arms on the table, shirtsleeves rolled up to his elbows.

'What's happening?' I asked.

My mother replied: 'Leave us alone, please.' I went back to my room.

'Can I offer you some coffee?' I heard her say.

One of them replied: 'No.'

The kitchen door was closed. My father said, in a loud voice, a tinge of sarcasm: 'You didn't have to come. You already know who I am. Or so you think.'

Shortly afterwards I saw my mother go into her room. She removed her palm dress, dropped it on the bed and put on a different one. She picked up my father's good shoes and a pair of socks from the chest of drawers. She stared at the open wardrobe for a bit.

'Mum?'

She came to me.

'What do they want?'

'They want to have a talk with Dad. I'm going, too. I'll call you as soon as I can. We'll be back soon, you'll see.'

I followed her. He was outside, barefoot on the porch, his back facing me, against the white light of morning. The two *carabinieri* looked like they were holding him up.

'He needs to put on his shoes,' she said.

My father whispered something in the younger one's ear, laughed and turned round, saw me, smiled at me, as if he was leaving for a journey that for so long he'd only imagined.

Anna listened to me as I told her what had happened.

'So what did you hear?' I asked.

She hesitated, cleared her throat. 'Just that something had happened.'

She thought I knew everything, which is why she'd called. She thought she'd have to tell me: 'I'm sorry.'

'You'll see it's nothing,' she added.

I could hear noises in the background.

'Where are you calling from?' I asked.

'The phone box,' she said, even though they now had a working line in the house. *Because of Stefano*, I thought. 'Really, you'll be fine.'

The light dimmed, the shutters of one of the windows slammed because of the wind. I looked at the wall in the rising shadow, and the bag in the van came back to me, the arms and neck and face of my father, the way he'd said: 'You already know who I am.'

'Elia?'

That's when I started *seeing* everything – imagining it, first just a vague sketch, then in more detail, as if she, unintentionally, had opened my eyes. As if it were written on the palm of a hand. *You need to believe in it*. Something that would sweep our lives away, that would separate and scatter us.

'Elia, are you still there? Hello?'

Ida came back later.

I'd had some cold spaghetti, smoked a couple of cigarettes, lain down on the sofa and dozed off.

It had started raining hard.

I opened the door. Ida shook her umbrella, Simona behind her with a bag in her hands, her head hanging down under a waterproof hood.

'Were you sleeping?' asked Ida.

I said yes.

'Have you seen this weather?' The kitchen was dark, and she went to switch on the lights. 'That's better,' she said, over the noise of the rain.

She ran her fingers through her hair, looking at the dirty dishes on the table. She breathed in deeply and twisted her nose, as if my parents' absence had created a bad smell. She was wearing a lumpy sweater that reached down to her knees.

Simona got a colouring book and a pencil case out of her bag. Ida moved a chair, told her: 'Take your coat off.' Then she added: 'Wait here, I need to talk to Elia.'

I wanted to go to my room, lock the door, but I let her come close, touch my arm, point at the hallway.

'Let's go through there a second.'

So I went back into the lounge.

'Sit down,' she said, and stood where she was, rubbing her hands. 'Your mother called me.'

'Why not me? Are they coming back?'

'I'm afraid not,' she replied, then came next to me, kneeled down and put her hands on my shoulders. 'Not yet.'

'What has he done?' I asked.

I'd thought about it all afternoon, before falling asleep. I'd gone back into the yard, climbed into the van, clutched that bag in my arms.

She shook her head.

'Your mother wants you to come and stay with me.'

'No.'

'You can't be alone.'

'I said no.'

She pulled me to her and stroked my head, as if I'd started crying and she was trying to console me. Her hands were cold, but her face was too hot. I tried resisting, arms stiff, fists closed. I gave up and hugged her.

'There you are,' she murmured.

My mother came back in the middle of the night.

Lying on the sofa in Ida's lounge, I hadn't been able to fall asleep: I was watching the rain hit the window, in the endless darkness, Simona's drawings pinned to the walls, the stereo on a shelf, the speakers, the changeable shadows of the trees across the ceiling. I was thinking about the last thing Anna had said – 'I'm here if you need me.' I was thinking of Ida's silences, over dinner, the way she kept looking at her watch and at the phone. I was thinking of my parents, and I wondered if they were next to each other, or separate. I imagined rooms and closed doors.

At some point, Ida joined me. She was in her pyjamas, rubbing her eyes. 'You're awake,' she said.

'So are you.'

'Are you comfortable?'

'Yes.'

'OK. Call me if you need anything.'

She was trying to make me feel less alone.

I curled up, hands between my legs, then I saw the head-lights cutting through the darkness, the rain, heard the click of a car door and the shrill sound of the bell.

Ida came back into the lounge and opened the door. I sat up as my mother walked in. Ida was holding her, saying: 'Look at you, you're soaked.' Then: 'Elia's here.'

They hugged there, in the dark.

I wanted to think that my father had stayed in the car, that he had said: 'I'll wait here,' and she had come in to get me. I tried believing that everything was fine, that he'd done something wrong, but he'd apologised and that had been enough.

'Come,' said Ida. 'I'll make you some coffee.'

My mother stayed silent.

Ida disappeared into the hallway, came back with a towel, handed it to her and went into the kitchen, switched on the light and turned on the tap.

'Sit down,' she told her.

In the dim light, my mother rubbed her hair. I felt she didn't really know where she was, that she didn't realise I was there. She ran the towel behind her neck and over her face, then let it fall and kneeled down. It was my mother, but she was turning into someone I didn't know. That was when it happened.

'Mum?' I said.

Simona woke up and Ida went to her room.

'Mum?'

I should've got up, but I couldn't.

She looked at me, eyes wide, a hand over her mouth. She started sobbing.

XIV.

The girl is standing perfectly still.

You look at the wire binding her wrists, as if it were a beautiful sight, almost moving. You can't think any more.

You can't stop saying: Come back down. Don't make me get up.

But she steps forward.

There's no point in trying to run. There's nothing left. Maybe there used to be, but there's nothing now. Maybe I dreamed it.

You turn over to one side. You look at the beginning of the path, as if the man had come back to help you, but now you know the truth. The sky is black, the wind hisses through the branches.

Listen, you say. We'll hide out here for a bit. I can take your hand, if you want. I can free you.

And she steps forward again.

So you close your eyes and count, slowly, up to five, then you continue. When you feel stronger, when you have stopped counting, you'll get up and catch her again and the girl will let herself be dragged back. You will free her, you will undress her and the two of you will be equals and you will no longer worry.

And while you have your eyes shut – eight, nine, ten – you picture your family, and you feel sorry, or maybe not. No one can tell.

I'm Here

That morning, in a grey, cool light, I ran to the bus stop and caught the bus into town.

The driver studied me, narrowing his eyes, as if my appearance held something he couldn't work out.

I greeted him and he waved back at me.

When I reached the last row, before sitting down, I looked out of the back window: the road studded with puddles, the woods and restaurant almost floating there, in mid-air.

The locked door of the shelter.

Where the car was usually parked, just an empty space.

I walked along the pavement around the house, worried I wouldn't find them, that they'd disappeared – the unreachable place I'd imagined Anna to be the previous day, talking to her on the phone, even though she'd said: 'I'm here.'

On the grass, on top of a plastic sheet, there were several

cans of paint, brushes, a dirty roller, and wet newspapers. A stained ladder was leaning against the wall.

The sky looked like it was curving and plunging down behind the trees.

My heart stopped and started again: it had kept doing that since my mother had sat sobbing in Ida's lounge, covering my hands with hers.

I waited and listened, but heard no noise. The door and windows were shut. I knocked, as a sliver of pale blue blossomed between the clouds, then I rapped against the window and squashed my nose to it.

Then I heard her: 'I'm coming.' She appeared in the hallway, saw me, and stopped. I returned to the door and she turned the key in its lock.

'Elia,' she said. 'Come in.'

The kitchen smelled of plastic, fresh paint and vinegar. The chairs on the table, legs up.

She looked me in the eyes, then turned to the hob, put on some coffee. 'Take a seat,' she said. She was wearing a pair of shorts, a white cardigan and leather sandals. She squeezed her elbows and smiled. Our eyes kept locking and darting away, until we were both sitting in front of a cup of coffee.

'You didn't sleep, did you?'

I shook my head. She looked tired, too.

'Drink, it'll go cold,' she said.

'Is Stefano not here?'

'They went to buy a new TV. They left about ten minutes ago.'

There were no electronics stores in Ponte, so I imagined them in the car, driving up the highway.

'Big news,' she said and looked away. 'I mean, it looks like they're getting along.'

I'd had the feeling for a while now – since the evening we kissed – that life was a constant push, and that something like that, the fact that it couldn't stop, not for anyone, the fact that it just kept flowing, would keep me afloat somehow.

'I'm glad.'

Anna pulled her hair back. 'Sorry. You have a thousand things on your mind and I'm just here talking.' She went to the window, looked out into the garden. 'How's your mother?'

'Bad. I don't know.'

She'd lain down on Ida's bed and slept on and off next to her. She'd woken up at dawn – I heard them whisper – and she'd come back into the lounge. Ida had lent her a sweater. She'd had a sip of water and sat back down on the edge of the sofa.

'It's stopped raining,' she'd said.

It seemed important to her, at the time.

'I need to go back over there. I can't take you. And even if I could, I wouldn't. This is something you need to forget about,' she'd said. *Did she really think I could forget?*

I'd watched her pick up her bag, put on her shoes and walk out, leaving me on the sofa, where she hoped I was safe.

Anna pressed a finger against the glass, the sky clearing up, sharper and more defined.

'It seems he hurt a girl,' I said, the only thing my mother, sobbing, had been able to voice. 'I know her. Everyone does.'

She nodded. 'I know, darling.'

Darling, as if I was also her son.

I squeezed my legs and closed my eyes. For a second there was just darkness, my father's eyes and his van, then the light came back, she was in front of me and I told her about the bag, I told her I'd taken it, taken it into the garage and hidden it on the highest shelf of the metal scaffold, where my father kept random stuff. As if no one could find it there. As if that was a task he'd given me, while they were taking him away, when he'd smiled at me like that.

Anna took my hands in hers.

'I hate him,' I said.

'You love him. And your father loves you. You have nothing to do with this. And there is nothing you can do.'

Her lips trembled with the beginning of a smile.

'You'll be happy, I told you, even though you can't believe it right now.' Then she turned my hands over and looked at them. 'It says so here. But this is *your* life, not anyone else's.'

Light had begun to flood the kitchen. I thought of my mother, sitting in a room, waiting for her husband, that indecipherable man.

I started crying, then apologised.

'Don't apologise. You'll see, things will sort themselves out.'

'How?'

'Come with me,' she said.

She took me into the new room – just a bed and a bedside table – where the shutters were half closed. She made me lie down, took off my shoes and socks and lay down next to me. I wanted to stop crying, I was ashamed. I turned towards the wall.

She said: 'Hey.' Then quiet. She brushed the hair off my forehead, then rested her hand on it, as if checking for a fever.

'Do you want to be alone?'

I said no, and turned to look at her.

She took off her sandals and let them fall, pushed her feet against mine, rubbed them. I rested my hand on her knee, at the line of her shorts.

'Stay here,' I said.

'Of course.'

'Don't go.'

She wiped away my tears, stroked my hair.

'What can I do?' she asked, and I moved closer, my nose running, feeling her warmth, and I kissed her on the mouth.

She moved.

'Don't you want to talk?' she asked.

'No.'

I just wanted to hold her, to get rid of that darkness and of my father.

'Can I touch you?'

Anna wrinkled her lips and lowered her eyes. 'OK,' she said.

I kneeled on that creaky bed, on top of the rough sheet that smelled of soap. I unbuttoned her cardigan, she stretched her arms and raised her back and I removed it – a white bra.

'Do you feel better?' she asked.

'Yes.'

I took off my T-shirt and lowered both her straps, the narrow, tiny shoulders, her breastbone under almost see-through skin.

She sat up, unfastened it, let it slide onto her stomach and used her hands to cover herself.

'Like this?' she asked.

'I want to see,' I said.

She opened her fingers and I glimpsed her nipples, and she half closed her eyes. 'It should be you doing it,' she murmured.

She moved her hands, placed them on the bed, and I caressed them.

We undid our trousers, lowered them to our ankles, we

freed ourselves and stopped. I told her she was beautiful – the white knickers, the loose elastic – and she shook her head, then lay down again and opened her legs to run them around my hips.

'I want to erase everything,' she said, pressing her hands against my chest, so I leaned over and we kissed. I stayed inside her mouth and around her tongue. As we broke off, out of breath, she took me by the shoulders and I lay down on top of her.

I asked her if I was heavy, and Anna said, 'No.'

With her feet resting against the back of my knees, I began to move.

'I'd like to know what it feels like,' she said. She was staring at a spot on the ceiling – *what was she talking about?*

'Do you want me to stop?'

She smiled. 'Do you?'

'No.'

'But don't rush. That's not how it should be.'

But I was rushing, as the room vanished. I felt like my head was emptying, like that bucket of dirty water she'd emptied the evening I spent the night there.

'I can't,' I whined, and I came.

When she returned from the bathroom she had a roll of toilet paper: she handed it to me, picked up her stuff and got dressed in silence.

I dried myself off. Anna gave me my jeans and T-shirt. I didn't know what to do with that piece of paper, so I stuffed it in one of my pockets. She touched her lips, as if they were bleeding, then lay down again, taking my hand, resting it on her breasts.

'What are you thinking about?'

'You,' I replied.

I could feel her heart beating.

'It feels like it's still night,' she said.

Time rewound itself – I saw the two of us, lying on that bed, then my mother, soaked with rain, the girl's bag on the top shelf, my father smiling on the porch.

'I don't know why, but I knew it,' she murmured.

'What?'

She didn't reply.

I curled up on one side: she was still, eyes shut. I wanted to start over again, even though I was exhausted, to free my hand and move it between her legs, but when I tried and she didn't move, I realised she'd fallen asleep.

What I remember is her profile, her slightly open mouth. A final moment of happiness, because we were there, we were close. Probably the wind. Then I fell asleep, too.

That's why we didn't hear them come back – the car on the tarmac and their footsteps on the pavement.

We woke again when the door opened and he walked in whistling. The fridge door, glass clinking.

Anna bolted up. I heard her whisper: 'Oh God.'

I thought we'd slept for ages, but it had only been half an hour since I'd arrived.

Stefano stopped whistling: he must've heard something.

She moved her legs, placed her naked feet on the floor. I slid across the mattress and sat up. He appeared at the door. He was holding a bottle by its neck. He peered into the half-light.

'What are you doing?' he asked.

Anna walked up to him. 'You already back? So, how did it go, did you get it? Where's your grandfather?'

'It was shut,' he said. 'We came back.' He kept staring at me, over his mother's shoulders.

'That's a shame. Come, let's get a glass.'

She disappeared into the hallway.

He took a step forward, eyes on me, then followed her.

Left alone – I could hear her voice but not his – I picked up my socks, put them on, put on my shoes. I wanted to lie down again, cover myself with the sheet, but I went into the kitchen.

Anna was leaning against the table, staring at the floor. She turned slightly, face undone and pale. Outside the open door, the paint cans and the grass shining under the sun.

'Where did he go?' I asked her.

*   *   *

He was sitting on the bonnet of the rusty car.

He didn't turn around as I walked towards him, nor when I sat down next to him.

Santo Trabuio appeared on the forecourt, greeted me with more warmth than usual and went into the kitchen.

'I know what happened to you,' said Stefano. 'I tried calling last night, and today.'

'I wasn't home.'

'I got that.'

He folded his left arm and touched his bicep. His laughter echoed through my head.

'I need a cigarette,' he said to himself. Then added: 'You'd better get away from here.'

'OK.'

There was nowhere I wanted to go back to, but I didn't say that. He got off the bonnet, walked with purpose to the trees at the end of the garden, then crouched down, sitting on his heels.

'So, what were you doing?' he asked, looking out towards the river.

'Nothing.'

He snorted and chuckled, stood up again, looked at the house. 'There she is,' he said.

I turned around and saw no one – closed door, light shining against the glass.

'I asked you what the fuck you were doing.'

'I was looking for you,' I replied, my voice weak.

That wasn't entirely accurate, but it was true.

'And how did you end up on that bed?'

He came back towards me. I jumped off the bonnet and made to leave, but he grabbed me by the elbow, squeezed it, and said: 'Look.' As if he were about to add something but then wasn't sure.

'Get off me.'

He raised a hand, holding it up between us.

'What? We're friends, aren't we? I just want to know.'

I stayed silent. He started walking back and forth, then stopped one step away from me.

'You shouldn't have,' he said.

He shoved me and I fell, he climbed on top of me and raised his fist to my face.

'I'm going to beat the shit out of you,' he whispered. 'I'm going to hurt you.'

Maybe this was the hardest part: life running on and pushing us forward, each along our own path.

'What, I shouldn't do it because you're in a pile of shit? Because your father is a fucking crazy person? Is that what you're thinking? *Poor little thing*.'

I wasn't.

'What, are you like him?'

He pressed his fist against my nose: at that moment, I heard the door open, slamming against the wall, and Stefano bolted upright.

His mother's voice across the garden: 'Stop it, the both of you.'

He looked at me one last time.

He could've hit me, but he got up, rubbed his hands against each other and patted them on his T-shirt.

'Never show your face around here again,' he said, leaving. 'Out of the way,' I heard him growl at her.

I sat up and looked their way: there she was, barefoot on the step, hands to her mouth. She came towards me, just a couple of uncertain steps, looked up to the sky and then turned round, doing what was right.

XV.

He brings the dog to the middle of the woods.

He has a rope with him.

I don't know how old he is – a kid.

The dog jogs next to him: wagging its tail, brushing his legs, licking his hand. Sometimes it falls back, sniffing the ground, but he can still hear its voice.

I know what's going on in that little head of yours.

I see things you can't even imagine.

He keeps walking, leaving home behind.

Splashes of sun and shade along the track. Dark and light, as always.

In a small clearing he runs the rope around a tree, ties it, calls it: 'Come here', slapping a hand on his knee, and tightens it around its neck.

He looks at it – tail still wagging, trustful, sniffing the grass, a pile of leaves, the scent of boar and fox, then it starts pulling and shaking its head to bite the rope. It settles down, muzzle between its paws.

He hears that voice become a whine.

What. Are. You. Doing?

He scratches its ears and strokes its back.

'Nothing.'

The dog closes its eyes.

He'd like to lie down next to it, fall asleep and find himself elsewhere when he wakes up, in his room or in the yard, looking for his dog, and maybe he will – most times he'll only remember burying it and a man just behind him, as he digs through his tears, asking himself: *Who could've done this?* But the doubt will slide into his sleepless nights, years later, at the wheel of the van, as he sits on the porch and the people who love him and whom he loves walk by him, talking and smiling, and he will reply or maybe not, staring at a wall or the edge of the woods, the darkness and its call, holding his secrets in his hands.

After

There are days when I think it was just a dream: my return home, the stretch of road I walked, the empty spot where my father parked his van, a patrol car next to my mother's. The garage was open: a *carabiniere* walked out of it, the still man from the kitchen. He lit a cigarette and looked at me, as I got closer. Someone else was moving inside, I could almost see them.

'Your mother was looking for you,' he said.

I didn't like his expression and his tone of voice – as if the world had mocked him without him deserving it. When he lifted his hat and wiped off the sweat, I saw a red birthmark on his forehead.

'Where's my father?' I asked.

Another *carabiniere* appeared at the door, shading his eyes, then stepped back into the garage.

The man just took a couple of drags, threw down the cigarette and squashed it with his heel. 'It's better if you go in.'

I knew I wouldn't find him at home. But, for a second, I thought my father had come back, that he was with my mother, that that was the point: they were worried. I hoped they'd let him go – just an accident, a case of mistaken identity – even though I felt like life, without him around, would be easier.

The bag came back to mind, the bag I'd hidden. How could I think they wouldn't find it?

The man had followed me with his eyes: before going in I nodded at him and he responded.

If I'd come in time, I thought, I would've taken the bag into the middle of the woods, as far away from home as possible, I would've dug a hole to hide it in, covering it with soil and twigs and leaves. Not for my father, I would've done it for myself.

What this says about the person I was back then, I can't explain.

Their bedroom door was open: on the floor, a pile of clothes and sheets.

My mother was sitting on my bed, elbows on her knees, face in her hands. She didn't turn round when I appeared at the door. I said hi. She glanced at me. She was still wearing Ida's sweater.

'I can't worry about you, too,' she said.

I went to open the window, that expanse of blue and the grass and the woods, the world I thought I knew. I could hear voices and footsteps from the garage.

'What did you do?' She pointed at my T-shirt. 'You're filthy.'

'I fell.'

'Where?'

'Doesn't matter,' I said. 'Dad?'

She brought a hand to her stomach. I stayed by the window, in a small puddle of light.

The voices were coming from outside, now: 'Here it is.'

My mother looked at me: 'Your father told them, Elia.'

He'd been quiet for most of the evening, indifferent to the questions being asked of him.

I never found out what made him talk, all of a sudden, or how he felt at that moment. There were the facts, or those that my father thought were the facts. The man following them in the car, a person he wouldn't name. The dash through the woods. The stream. The moment he'd tied up the girl, taped her mouth – only to protect her. The conspiracy. The letters he'd written and which, he claimed, had brought him a lot of unwanted attention.

His fear and then his anger. His anger and then his exhaustion.

What is left of my father is what we call a confession, as if he'd chosen to reach out a hand that no one had wanted to take, nobody but her, my mother.

*　　*　　*

221

'He did it, Elia. He said so.'

She looked through her swollen eyes at the unlit light on the ceiling.

'Sit here,' she told me.

I sat down and she stroked my shoulder.

'I can't believe it. Even though I know it's true.'

'Me neither,' I replied, but I did believe it.

There was the sound of a car door closing and footsteps on the porch. The man knocked, called out to my mother. She patted her skirt, answered: 'I'm coming.' She walked unsteadily towards the bedroom door. Her legs gave way and she clung onto the frame.

'Mum?'

'I've got it.'

I could've helped her, but I didn't want to see him. I imagined him as he held up the bag, asking me: 'Do you know anything about this?' Staring at me, as if my father and I were no different.

They spoke in hushed voices. Before leaving, he said: 'Believe me, we're sorry.'

I joined her after a bit: she was watching the patrol car disappear behind the trees.

'He was kind,' she said.

'What difference does it make?'

'There are people who only see the bad things in this world, and behave accordingly. That man doesn't. That's the difference. And you mustn't become one.'

'What did he say to you?'

She pulled the sweater down over her legs.

'They found her bag. It was hidden in the garage.'

That afternoon the phone never stopped ringing.

She answered every time.

'I'll get this,' she'd say.

It was easy to figure out who she was talking to: Ida, because she let herself go and cried; old colleagues of my father's and the construction manager; a journalist from the *Eco della Valle* to whom she said, 'I have nothing to add', and who phoned again, a couple of minutes later. Twice, there was only silence on the other end of the line, and she raised her voice: 'Don't you have a scrap of heart?' – I wasn't sure, but I thought it might be Anna.

Then that last call came.

I was eating some biscuits, sitting at the table, in the kitchen. It was sunset by now. I stood up and went into the hallway; she came out of the bathroom, still unsteady, reached the small table, picked up the receiver, said: 'Hello?' She burst into tears.

It was my father.

'Sweetheart, how are you? Where are you now?'

They'd moved him: he wasn't at the station, next to the town hall, where I could still picture him.

'We can fix things. Make them understand. Try making them understand.'

My father said something and she smiled through her tears: for a second she became the woman she'd always been, as if her character – her nature – were inevitably tied to that of my father and destined to disappear if he did.

'I know,' she said. 'Wait.' She turned to me, beckoned me over, handed me the phone. I didn't have the courage to tell her I didn't feel like talking to him.

'Dad?'

Silence. A metallic noise, wherever he was now, keys in a lock. I looked at my mother, tried again: 'Dad?'

'Elia?'

'Yes it's me.'

'How are you?'

'Fine.' I don't know why I said that.

Laughter in the background. My father lit a cigarette and started coughing.

'I can't think any more, you know? I can't figure out where I am. Where are you?'

'Home. You called home.'

My mother pressed a hand against my back, holding me or herself up.

'Stay there then,' he said. 'Stay there. Don't leave.'

Before saying goodbye, he told me something else.

'You know that time we went out together? That night? It just came back to me.'

We didn't *go out*, I thought. *You dragged me outside.*

'The worst part is going out there alone,' he said.

'Where?'

He didn't reply immediately. And then he didn't explain what he meant.

'I didn't want to hurt anyone, but it looks like I did.'

'Yes, Dad.'

'I need to go now. Bye.'

'What did he say?' asked my mother, as I hung up.

'Nothing.'

Lying on my bed, I was trying to fall asleep.

Simona was drawing, on the lounge floor. Ida was talking with my mother. 'We can stay here if you want,' she suggested.

She'd brought over some dinner and washed the dishes. She'd hugged me and kissed my head, before I went into my room.

My mother said no: she had to get through this alone – though she'd often ask her to stay after that.

She walked with them to the top of the drive – their voices growing weaker, in the dark. Everything went quiet, and I imagined my father at the end of the garden – *What do you want from me?* Then I saw Anna again holding my hips with her legs and Stefano pinning me to the ground, fist raised. Our cries at the falls, as we jumped into the water, the place where my father had taken the girl – though I didn't know that yet.

My mother came back in, locked the door. I heard her
sigh, opening a cupboard, then something smashing onto
the floor and her shouting: 'Why?'

I ran to the kitchen: she was staring at a broken plate.
She picked up a couple of shards and threw them into the
bin.

'I didn't mean to shout. Did I wake you up?'

'I wasn't asleep.'

'I didn't mean to anyway.'

'Never mind. I'll go back to my room.'

'Sit here for a bit,' she said, and we both sat down.

'What is it?' I asked her, impatiently, but she either
didn't notice or didn't care.

'I told you once that you shouldn't feel disappointed.'

'So?'

There was nothing that could've comforted me then.

'So it can change your life, I think. Not feeling disappointed. Not now. Maybe not now. But it's something you
need to think about.'

She turned towards the door and then back to me, studying me.

'Disappointment keeps you tied to the wrong things,'
she said. 'People expect you to drop everything, when
things go wrong. So . . .'

She stood up, opened the door again and switched on
the porch light, as if he were out there. She looked into the
darkness.

'I always loved him. I can't even remember not loving him. This is what should tie you to people, Elia. Love. Everything else is just what we tell ourselves we deserve, and it doesn't mean much, most of the time.'

She gestured with a kind of wave.

'I've thought about some things, you know? I don't know why they felt so important. They don't matter at all now. You have your life to live. And I need to stay here.'

I left my mother to imagine him, in the dark, talking to him in silence, with kindness, despite the horrible things he'd done.

It was raining again when I woke up.

I slipped into my grassy, soil-stained jeans and T-shirt, went to the bathroom, then into the kitchen.

Ida was sitting down. Simona was staring at the rain running down the glass. Ten in the morning.

'Your mother was awake until just a few minutes ago,' said Ida. 'She's sleeping now. What do you want for breakfast?'

I said I wasn't hungry.

'Not even a cup of *caffellatte*?'

'Yeah, maybe a bit.'

I watched her move between the fridge and the sink, practical and sure in that mess.

'Hello,' I said to Simona, and she came close to me and did something I wasn't expecting: she took my hand, scrunched up her lips and frowned, as if she felt a pain she couldn't express.

'Hey,' I said. 'Thanks.'

She pulled back, but kept looking at me.

Ida put a mug on the table.

'Go on,' she said.

My mother called her.

'I'll be back in a second.'

I drank my *caffellatte*, as Simona continued to watch me.

'Shitty situation, isn't it, Tex?' I said, imitating Stefano's voice. 'Shitty situation.' I walked out into the damp, cool air, the porch light still on. A sour gag rose up from my stomach as I stepped into the yard. I reached the postbox. Where could I go? I was cold and wet, in tears.

Stop it, I told myself.

Then I saw a car on the side of the road.

The windscreen was fogged up. The lights flickered on and off, the wipers pushed the water away, and I ran towards her.

What I can tell you is that I was sixteen, that summer, and she was thirty-six. That my father had kidnapped a girl and they'd arrested him. That my only friend had found me in bed with his mother. That Anna shouldn't have been there, and that we didn't talk for a long while. That, at a certain point, she took my hand and I asked: 'Does Stefano know you came here?' and she shook her head. That he'd shouted at her the previous day, he'd left the house slamming the door behind him, and when he'd got back he'd gone straight to his room. That they hadn't eaten. That she'd taken the car just to calm down but then drove all the way up here. That she'd considered leaving, but stayed.

'I should've,' she said.

She had kept her left hand on the wheel, as if she were about to leave. 'How is . . . ?' she asked.

'I heard him on the phone yesterday.'

'I meant your mother.'

I shrugged.

'Where were you going?'

'I have no idea,' I replied.

She smiled, let my hand go and tapped hers on her knee. I leaned over and rested my head on her lap.

'No one is the same, Elia. Your father is just himself.' She traced the outline of my ear with a finger. 'He was so sad sometimes, I told you. Like he was closed off in his world, locked inside. I think I saved his life, once.'

She told me about the falls, as she stroked my hair, about when he'd jumped into the water and wouldn't come back up.

'I never told anyone. Now you know. Maybe I shouldn't have, but it's the truth.'

The rain ran down the windscreen and windows.

'I'm sure he's done everything he could since then, to not let himself go, to be with you.'

'I don't care,' I said.

'That's not true. That's what hurts.' She bent over and kissed my cheek. 'It was nice,' she murmured.

'What?'

'Yesterday.'

I thought about happiness for a second. I thought about the river and the plant, the cold chimneys and the slope, the beach and the falls, and I had the feeling I'd never really looked at them. An abandoned place where rain had been falling for years.

'I want to stay here with you,' I said.

She reached for the dashboard and started the engine.

'It was nice.' Then she moved her legs as if I were a weight she was forced to remove. 'Now go back to your mother.'

I got out of the car and watched her, in the pouring rain, as she turned it around and drove off.

XVI.

I only imagined it – my father and the girl, the things they told each other, the things he said and thought. What he thought he'd seen. Because the story of my father is partly *my* story too. And it's the story of my mother, almost all of it. But what happened after the girl was able to stand up and walk away in the dark, unsteady on her feet, what my father did then, that's much more difficult to imagine.

It was my mother who told me about a man on the path. My father had told her about it, during a visit. He told her he'd met him before, and when and where – 'You know that's not true, Ettore.' But what they said to each other, as he was in the water, that is nothing but a daydream, and it belongs to me.

Ida was the one who told me it had happened at the falls. She told me about a stream and a pool – a place she didn't know – and I understood straight away. Those beer cans that Stefano had seen, by coincidence, behind the tree.

Someone else comes up here.

They found the knife: there was dried blood on the blade. They found the tape, the torch, her shoes and everything else. He hadn't even tried to get rid of them, just like he hadn't got rid of the bag.

He'd shown his arms to the *carabinieri*, when they came to our house. *Here I am*. He didn't resist.

I'm sure that's what he wanted.

Over There

Sometimes I was able to pretend he didn't exist, or that he was no longer my father. I'd find myself thinking of a December afternoon: we were shovelling, in the yard, and he had lain down in the snow we hadn't yet touched, opening his legs and arms, telling me that the shape he'd make, the shape of his body, would last until the end of winter.

'That's not possible, Dad.'

'You'll see.'

That same evening it started snowing again.

The shape had disappeared.

I'd stay closed up in my room, as my mother kept talking to Ida about what to do, bursting into tears, or calling the lawyer that Ida had suggested and paid for as we could no longer afford it.

The last time I saw him was in an intensive care room.

His cellmates said his eyes had suddenly gone wide, he'd brought his hands to his chest and collapsed.

He was taken to the hospital, where his heart stopped.
He was thirty-seven.

I'd heard him on the phone, a couple of days earlier. He was confused, slurring his words as if still half asleep. He coughed and stuttered, holding the phone away from his mouth.

Several times, he'd asked, 'And who are you again?'

'It's me, Dad.'

'Elia?'

'Yes.'

'Sorry, I got lost.'

My mother had gone to visit him, that Sunday – I still hadn't – and had come home saying he wasn't feeling well, he looked terrible and was refusing to eat: how could they still hold him in prison?

'You know why,' I told her.

'I'm not stupid, that's not what I mean.'

The judge had requested a psychiatric evaluation, to assess whether my father was fit for trial. He kept repeating the story of the car and the chase. He refused to describe the vehicle, he refused to say the man's name – 'I'd be putting you in danger.'

'I had a dream,' he said, suddenly, with his old voice. 'We were in the van, you and me and Mum. I knew where I was going and everything was fine. When I woke up, it felt real. But here I am.'

'It was just a dream.'

My father sighed.

'It's all the same to me.'

We rushed to the hospital, when they called us. The journey lasted forever, my mother kept repeating: 'Oh God.'

They only let us in for a couple of minutes, wearing scrubs and surgical masks. She bent over, in front of a machine that translated his heartbeat into weak waves of light and sound, then she pulled down her mask, whispered into his ear and grazed his lips with hers.

I didn't move any closer. I stayed far away from his bed, staring at my father's barely alive body under the sheet, my mother's back. Later, she would say it had been a precious moment, and that she was sure he'd felt our presence in the room, that he'd held on, forcing his heart to keep beating so he could see us again, so he could keep a final memory of the people he loved the most in the world, so he didn't have to leave alone.

He died shortly after.

They tried resuscitating him, without success.

We were in the corridor, waiting. I was watching the prison officer shift his weight from one leg to the other.

My mother spoke to the doctors, holding my hand, then told them she wanted to see him again.

She seemed smaller and faded, when she came back out.

'He's gone now.'

We went home. I watched the road and the cars, the sky low and dark. My mother sobbed. I couldn't figure out what had happened, it didn't feel real. I just sat there, going through places I didn't recognise.

She stopped along a straight road, turned off the engine and got out. I followed her with my eyes as she moved away, then I got out, too. The air was cold, the river at our feet. I saw a plastic bag being dragged by the current.

'Just give me a minute,' she said.

That was when, as I stared at the water, I thought about the last thing my father had said, on the phone, just as I was about to hang up.

'You still there?'

'Yes, Dad.'

'Did you go and take a look?'

'I don't understand.'

'Over there.'

'Over there where?'

'Never answer a question with another question.'

XVII.

Whatever he'd thought of doing to the girl – when he'd offered her the lift, when he'd told her about the chase, forced her to walk along the path, tied her and gagged her and forced her to lie down next to his naked body – my father never did it, and let her go.

That's what happened.

He stayed off to one side, and she got away.

I've often imagined her stumbling barefoot along the path, branches lashing her face, rocks and roots under her feet, terrified, sure he'd be coming for her, that he'd use the knife, then finding herself where he'd parked the van.

I imagine her looking around and walking along the middle of the lane, a ghostly figure, towards the barking dog, towards the light – the house where they rescued her – and everything that followed, before dawn and as the sun rose.

And I imagine my father: he got dressed, threw his shoes

into the water and returned to the van. He didn't see her along the road they'd come from: she was safe.

When my mother told me about the bag, I kept the truth to myself.

'Why did he put it there? What was the point?' she asked, and I didn't reply.

Maybe it would've helped her to know my father wasn't responsible – not for that, at least – that he hadn't tried hiding it, but I never found the courage.

Truth (2)

Not many people came to the funeral, on a cold, grey morning. A couple of colleagues from the plant, some labourers and builders from the site, Ida and Simona, two women from the library. Sitting at the very back, alone, Santo Trabuio, in a suit and shirt buttoned all the way up to his neck. After the ceremony, he left.

My mother took me by the elbow, in the cemetery, pointed at the coffin and murmured: 'Look at your father.' Her legs gave in and Ida held her up, as they slid the coffin into the wall.

When we got home she stayed very still, just one step in from the door.

'I don't know what to do without him,' she said.

Ida helped her to the bedroom, helped her to get out of her clothes and came back into the kitchen.

'Sit down a moment,' she said, and told me about my mother, the pressure she'd been shouldering, out of love, and her efforts to help him and protect me at the same time.

'You'll have to grow up fast now. Your father—'

'I hate him,' I cut her short. 'I don't want to be his son.'

'That's not true, you know that. And hate does nothing. It never helps anyone. Maybe that's what you can learn now.'

Years later I would thank her for those words.

'I tried. I'm still trying.'

She looked at me, tapping her fingers against her chin. 'I think my memory's starting to play tricks on me.'

She was almost seventy. Slow and heavy, but still capable of suffocating you with a hug and bursting out laughing.

And that's what she did, then, and said: 'I really don't remember telling you that.'

She'd erased it and moved on. That wasn't her life, after all: it was mine, and it had been *my* summer, my family's summer.

I went back to school the following week.

My classmates were kind, but they avoided me if they could: I didn't care. I just went back home, after class, hoping no one would notice me. The son of Ettore Furenti.

They gave us back the van and we sent it to the scrapyard.

His clothes, on the other hand, stayed in the wardrobe, his shaving cream, toothbrush and razor in the bathroom, his things in the garage.

Ida found another girl to help her out.

My mother went back to work at the library.

In the evenings we'd sit at the table and she'd stare at my father's empty seat, twisting her napkin, not touching her food. We didn't know what to say. We'd watch TV, my mother curled up on the sofa, me on the floor. On Saturdays I went with her into town and we bought food, though it was Ida, more often than not, who cooked our meals.

The phone kept ringing: once a voice asked me, in falsetto, if I was the son of the man who liked kidnapping women, and was I going to do it, too? One Sunday morning, a guy I thought I recognised said it was my father who'd killed the boy at the mine.

'Good thing he croaked,' he added, and hung up.

When I went back into the lounge, my mother was staring at the floor. 'Who was it?' she asked.

'No one.'

She made room for me next to her.

'What if it really was him?' I asked her.

'Who did what?'

'You know.'

'Look at me, Elia. Don't listen to them, whatever they might say. If that's what you're thinking about, stop it, because it's not true. You have nothing to be ashamed of.'

The following morning I gathered all my comics, took them into the yard, gathered them into a pile and burned them, watching the smoke rise in the cold autumn air – *It's just a bunch of shit, Tex*. I went back to my room, took down the boy's photo and threw that into the fire, too.

Winter came and it started snowing.

My mother fell ill. She had a high temperature and kept vomiting. She set a small bowl by her bed, got under the covers and called me.

'Can you go to the chemist's for me? Get me some aspirin,' she said, then turned onto one side, in pain.

I was walking out of the shop when I saw her – it hadn't happened yet and I had been dreading it. She didn't notice me straight away. She crossed the road and climbed over a pile of dirty snow. Her hair was short now, her face lean and sharp. She came towards me, lifted her head up and looked at me.

'Hello,' I said.

'Hi.' She started biting her lip.

'How are you?' A stupid question.

She raised her eyebrows. 'How are *you*?'

'OK.'

'That's OK, then.'

She ran a hand through her hair, as if she were trying to untangle it, a gesture I still remembered, one that survived from that night with my father, and I saw her step out of the bus, huffing and yawning, and in Ida's garden, lying in the sun in her bra – the rip I couldn't sew back together.

She looked away.

'I just wanted—' I said.

She shook her head. 'Can I get through, please?'

'Sorry,' I said, and moved out of the way.

One morning in January, a blue sky, snow on the drive. School hadn't started yet. My mother and I were having breakfast.

'I need to talk to you, Elia.'

She looked up and caught her breath.

'We need to sort things out. Your father's things. I open the wardrobe every morning and I see his things. I can't do it. I can't bear it.'

'OK.'

'I have to.'

'Yes, I know.'

'But I need your help.'

She finished her breakfast and went to get dressed. A couple of minutes later I joined her and she pointed at the wardrobe.

'We can take them down to the church,' she said.

'Fine by me.'

'The shoes, too. You should keep something.'

She started crying in silence.

I looked at my father's clothes: without thinking, I took out a sweater and a shirt. We put everything else into bags. My mother threw out some yellowing underwear and a couple of old pyjamas, then took the coat off its hanger.

'This one is staying with me,' she said, putting it on.

We went into the garage and looked around.

'What do we do with this?' she asked, touching the sofa, its torn fabric.

'Throw it out,' I replied.

We managed to drag it up to the road and left it next to the bins. She stepped back, in that giant coat, and took one final look at it.

Walking back, she took my arm. She'd lost the colour in her face, and she walked carefully. Patches of snow shimmered in the sun.

'Take a look at his tools. Decide what you want to do. Let's keep the heater, I want to put it by the bed.'

'I'll sort it out,' I told her.

Alone, in the garage, I had the impression that my father was there, in the shadows, watching me.

They searched everywhere already, so it's your turn now? I could hear him mumble.

'Leave me alone,' I replied.

There was a sink under the small window: I took a sip of water and rinsed my face. Under the sink, a small cupboard. I had no idea what was inside. I opened it: a pile of newspapers and a bag of salt for the drive. I put the newspapers on the floor – I would throw them out – then kneeled down, picked one up and leafed through it, and as I did, something fell out: it was a parcel, wrapped in the first page of an issue of the *Eco della Valle*, tied with string, a tight knot. In the top-left corner, my father had written in black pen: ME.

I found a pair of scissors, unwrapped the parcel and what I found left me breathless: a sheet of paper, ripped from a notebook, with TRUTH written on it, and twenty-one letters, envelopes sealed, addressed and stamped, the ones he'd sent off, or so I thought. The story of the conspiracy he'd wanted to reveal.

They had been there all along.

No one had received them.

My mother called me: 'Elia? Everything OK?'

I looked into the winter light, outside the garage door, the clear sky and the snow. And I remembered.

Did you go and take a look?

Where?

Over there.

When I showed them to her, my mother burst into tears.

She was crying and smiling and saying: 'See?'

She pulled out a chair and sat down, scattered them on the table, caressing them as if they were my father's body, then sent me to fetch a box where she kept a few small treasures, my grandmother's pendant and some old photos.

She put the letters in the box.

'I don't want to open them,' she said. And never did.

Life

Stefano left school, as he said he would.

One day my mother went to get petrol and saw 'that kid' coming out of the shelter, cigarette in his mouth, a filthy cloth stuck in a pocket.

'He was alone. I asked him about his grandfather, but I got no reply.'

He didn't know her. I wondered what he would've done if she'd introduced herself. Would he have told her he was sorry about my father? Would he have asked her how I was?

I don't think so. He wasn't the type to do that.

They moved back to the city at the end of February.

I went to the petrol station before they left, but I stopped by the phone box – *Never show your face around here again.*

Anna was at the open window: she looked in my direction, leaned forward, waved at me, and shut it.

*　　*　　*

I never went back to the falls.

I got through my school year without opening a book.

One evening in June I told my mother that I was going to a friend's birthday party, but instead I headed to *Il cacciatore*, which was empty and dark, and sat on the kerb, in the car park, staring at the windows and the shadow of the curtains inside.

I don't know how long I sat there. I picked up a rock, raised my arm, aimed at a window and threw it: the glass cracked.

I started running.

When I got home, my mother was lying on the sofa, the lights off.

'You back already?' she asked.

'I'm going to bed. I'm tired.'

During that summer, things got worse.

I'd go down to the beach but I stayed by myself, fully clothed, watching the others swim, sunbathe and laugh and kiss. Whenever someone tried talking to me – which was not that often – I barely replied.

I got beaten up by a big, hulking guy who'd just finished high school. I egged him on. He grimaced and said: 'You're just like your father.'

I jerked forwards, fists clenched and he launched himself at me, threw me down onto the pebbles and punched me in the face.

'Fucking stop it,' he shouted.

I told my mother it was my fault.

'That's not true,' she replied, pressing ice on my lips. It wasn't your fault, she repeated. It wasn't your father's fault. It wasn't anyone's fault. She kept saying it for years.

One morning I went back to the petrol station.

Santo Trabuio was sitting in the shelter, his chin on his chest. He looked asleep. The air was hot and still. He half-opened his eyes and looked at me.

'Come in. You want a smoke?'

He handed me his packet and I came closer, took one.

'What are you after?' he asked.

How could I tell him?

He studied the burning tip of his cigarette, then nodded, as if I'd asked him a question, and said: 'They're doing fine. We talk on the phone.'

He rubbed his stubbled cheeks. He started coughing, brought a handkerchief to his mouth, put out the cigarette in the overflowing ashtray. I did the same.

'I didn't mean to disturb you,' I said, and made to leave.

'Elia?'

He was looking at something just behind me, the petrol pumps, the road, the unkempt field – I saw some blood on the white fabric of his handkerchief.

'It's always you,' he said. 'Always asking about you.'

'Who?'

He stayed quiet for a second.

'You know who,' he replied, and added: 'Stay strong.'

He didn't have long left – he died six months later.

Walking away, I looked at the empty house and saw Anna again, as she was hanging out the laundry, humming, and Stefano sitting on the wall, in the warm wind and under the sun.

I left in 1982.

After finishing high school I worked at the furniture factory for a bit, coming home for dinner, finding my mother always waiting for me. She talked about my father a lot, memories and funny anecdotes. She'd put on weight, her eyes veiled behind her glasses.

'I miss him,' she kept saying.

I pretended to listen, but never really did. She nodded and smiled. She knew that I wanted to leave, and that I thought I had no other choice.

Then I found a job in a factory that made doors and windows, an hour and a half's drive from Ponte. It was a job like any other, a small town like any other. Another river, other woods. Another valley. It was fine.

It's what I still do. I live here now.

I've never been married and I don't have children. But I am with someone: she's divorced, works in accounting and has a ten-year-old son – smart, thoughtful kid. They sleep at my place at the weekends, and I stay awake, in the darkness, listening to her breathing, light and regular, and the creaking of the bed in the room next door. Sometimes he has nightmares, so we get up, and she lies down next to him, still half asleep, and murmurs: 'There there.' Holds him in her arms.

I stay in the doorway – their intimacy and all that warmth – then I go to the kitchen and smoke a cigarette.

I told her about my father, about Anna and her son, about that summer. She's the only one here who knows.

'I care about you,' she says.

'So do I.'

'I love you.'

'So do I.'

'You're not planning on running away, are you?' she asks me.

'How did you know? Did you see my bags packed?'

'Don't tease me.'

'Where on earth would I go?'

Where can I possibly go?

I rarely go back to Ponte.

I talk to my mother on the phone: she asks me about the kid – she likes him a lot, and she thinks he's a bit like me – and about when I'll go and visit.

'Are you OK, sweetheart?'

'Of course, Mum.'

'Ida and Simona say hi.'

'Say hi to them from me.'

I like this house, the empty garden. From the bedroom window you can see the river. I like reading – novels, like she did. I like staying up late, sitting on a sunbed in the garden, when it's too hot and I can't breathe inside. I drink a cold beer. I like the birds singing, before the sun rises. Sometimes, at dawn, after a sleepless night, I look at my left hand, the palm now rough and calloused, as if I were able to see what Anna saw that day – my happy life, my good life. Like a road I would take, she was sure of it, and then walk to its end, pushed forward by the wind blown from that summer, so long ago.

Are you not happy?

Who knows?

I think so. We're only people, Elia.

What is the truth, I asked myself, but never found an answer.

My father smiles, before disappearing.

Maybe he just wanted someone – me – one day to switch on a light, to see him clearly, and then let him go where he had to go.

I hope I did.

It's what we all want.

And then there are your memories, what you imagine, and your dreams, your ghosts. What you can't tell anyone. And while they sleep, at night, Anna walks into the kitchen, humming, in her cardigan and sandals, and Stefano sits on the table, nods at me, asks me: How's life, Tex?

You haven't changed, I tell them. I wanted to thank you, I say, but they never answer.

I look at them, as I finish smoking, then I go back to bed, and I see my father walk across the hallway. He appears at the bedroom door, in the half-light, looks around him, sits down next to me.

What do you still want? I ask him.

I'm only sixteen. It's summer. The house where we lived.

Can you hear me?

Get up, he answers. His hands are shaking. Come with me, now.

Where?

You'll see.

Why did you do it?

Because that's how it happened.

Was it you? The boy?

What kind of question is that?

Never answer a question with another question. You taught me that.

My father smiles at me. True.

Tell me, then.

It wasn't me.

The wind is blowing: it never stopped, in my mind, ever. I take his hands and squeeze them: they're slim and cold, they're my father's hands. I want him to stop shaking.

He's still a young man, and he's just a shadow on a path, or in a van, the shape of a body in the snow. I ask myself if that's all he ever was, if he knew that and couldn't bear it. Not at the end, in any case.

He takes his hands out of mine.

Your mother? he asks.

She's fine.

You sure you don't want to come?

I can't, sorry.

Are you angry with me?

Not any more, I don't think.

I did make you laugh, sometimes, he tells me.

Sometimes, yes.

Don't forget that.

I won't, Dad.

You sure?

Yes. Now go to sleep.

That's when he gets up, slowly.

Goodnight, he says. I'll see you soon.

I watch him leave into the darkness. I clutch at the blanket, as if this were enough. I wait for her to come back to bed, to lie down next to me. Small things. Her breathing, next to the whistling of the wind that only I can hear. The river flowing in the distance, and its music. The smell of night. The kindness that, despite everything, we give and receive. The good life. The life we have left, this is all it is, and we must not waste it.

Author's note

Can you hear me? is the story of Elia Furenti and his father Ettore. It's the story of one summer, and one night, in 1978.

It's also a lot more personal than that. Long before Elia came to light – an undistinguishable form to begin with, little more than a shadow – *Can you hear me?* was the story of my father, my own story, in the last few years of our time together.

My father was sick. He suffered from bipolar disorder. He was depressed and uncontrollable. He was a loser – that's what he would call himself, crying – and a megalomaniac. A good man, smart and funny, and yet frightful, obsessive, determined to buy a gun. I loved him and I didn't know him. He was right in front of me and I couldn't reach him anymore. That's when I began transforming reality into fiction.

We do what we can with what happens to us. Life takes many different forms, and in this form, through words, we have the chance to imagine what it was previously

Elena Varvello

unimaginable. We try to tell the story of what we can't understand.

If books can save lives, *Can you hear me?* saved mine . . .

I let them go, now, Elia and Ettore, and my father. I watch them leave. Wherever they might go, they are safe now. They are happy, in their own way.

And, more importantly, they are together.

Acknowledgments

Elena Varvello

I am grateful to Daniela Petracco (my friend of many years and my first reader), Charlotte Seymour and the whole of Andrew Nurnberg Associates: without you none of this would have been possible.

Special thanks to Federico Andornino, Kate Brunt, Amber Burlinson, Hannah Corbett, Lisa Highton, Sara Kinsella, Jess Kim, Ruby Mitchell, Aimee Olivier, Emma Petfield, Susan Spratt and Diana Talyanina, my new, wonderful Two Roads family: getting to know you has been a privilege and a total joy.

And finally, thank you to Alex Valente, whose translation made this journey possible. It's been a long trip, and we never travel alone.

Alex Valente

Danny, the one to blame.
Elena, for the eerie trip in the woods.
Fede, for the invaluable assistance.
Catherine, for crossing her own timeline.

About the author

Elena Varvello was born in Turin, Italy, in 1971.

After completing an MA in creative writing she published two collections of poetry, *Perseveranza è salutare* and *Atlanti*. Her short story collection *L'economia delle cose* was nominated for the prestigious Premio Strega (the Italian equivalent of the Man Booker Prize) and won both the Premio Settembrini and the Premio Bagutta Opera Prima. A short film of the same title has been based on the short story 'La pistola'. Her debut novel, *La luce perfetta del giorno*, was published by Fandango in 2011. *Can you hear me?* is her first novel to be translated into English.

Elena teaches creative writing at the Scuola Holden in Turin. She lives with her husband and two children in a small village in the woods, not far from her birthplace.

elenavarvello.com

About the translator

Alex Valente is a European half-Yorkshire, half-Tuscan freelance translator.

He has researched comics, poetry, and their translation, co-edits the *Norwich Radical*, regularly translates for Italian literary agencies, and does voluntary work for non-profit organisations.

He's on Twitter as @DrFumetts.

TWO
ROADS

stories ... voices ... places ... lives

We hope you enjoyed *Can you hear me?* If you'd like to know
more about this book or any other title on our list,
please go to www.tworoadsbooks.com

For news on forthcoming Two Roads titles,
please sign up for our newsletter

enquiries@tworoadsbooks.com

TwoRoadsBooks